"Hey!" Sam yelled. "What's that?"

She pointed to a gift-wrapped package at the side of the driveway. It was illuminated by the light coming from inside the house.

They ran over to it.

"There's a card on it," Sam said. She reached down and picked it up.

"'To Erin'" she read.

"Careful, it might be a bomb," Jake warned.

"Oh, come on!" Erin laughed. "You've seen too many movies!" Erin quickly tore open the wrapper and looked inside.

In it were a plastic container of a well-known diet shake mix, several Weight Watchers frozen entrees, and an article from a popular magazine entitled, "Lose Weight and Make a New You!" Taped to the top of the article was a note that read, "Hey, fatso, get a clue!"

"Diana De Witt," Sam muttered, her teeth clenched. "It has to be her. . . ."

Sunset Sensation

CHERIE BENNETT

Sunset™ Island™

SPLASH™

A BERKLEY / SPLASH BOOK

SUNSET SENSATION is an original publication of The Berkley Publishing Group. This work has never appeared before in book form.

SUNSET SENSATION

A Berkley Book / published by arrangement with General Licensing Company, Inc.

PRINTING HISTORY
Berkley edition / June 1994

All rights reserved.
Copyright © 1994 by General Licensing Company, Inc.
Cover art copyright © 1994 by
General Licensing Company, Inc.
This book may not be reproduced in whole or in part, by mimeograph or any other means, without permission.
For information address: General Licensing Company, Inc., 24 West 25th Street, New York, New York 10010.

A GLC BOOK

Splash and Sunset Island are trademarks belonging to General Licensing Company, Inc.

ISBN: 0-425-14253-1

BERKLEY®
Berkley Books are published by
The Berkley Publishing Group,
200 Madison Avenue, New York, New York 10016.
BERKLEY and the "B" design
are trademarks belonging to Berkley Publishing Corporation.

PRINTED IN THE UNITED STATES OF AMERICA

10 9 8 7 6 5 4 3 2 1

For J.G.,
my favorite person in the whole world

ONE

"You know, we ought to sunbathe topless," Sam Bridges suggested mischievously. She pulled down the tiny strap that held up the top of her blue-and-white string bikini and wiggled her eyebrows at her friends.

"Not in this lifetime," Carrie Alden, one of Sam's two best friends, replied with a shudder. She looked down at her own kelly green one-piece suit with the built-in bra and the crisscross straps across her back. "The day I sunbathe topless is the day I am fifteen pounds thinner and living alone on a desert island."

"Oh, come on," Sam wheedled. "Live dangerously. No one can see."

Emma Cresswell, Sam's other best friend, fiddled with the slender strap that held up the top of her modest but very expensive white bikini. "What about the yacht steward?" she asked. "There's no way that—"

Just then a very handsome, dark-haired, uniformed yacht steward poked his head out of a hatch in the boat and looked toward the bow deck.

"Can I get you girls anything?" he asked, a wry look on his face, as if he'd overheard the last exchange between Emma and Sam.

"Yeah, you and two friends as cute as you," Sam muttered, her head turned away from the steward, "and all three of you would be giving me and my two best friends here delicious back rubs."

Carrie snorted back a laugh, and Sam cracked up at her own wicked wit.

"Did I say something funny?" the steward asked, a bemused look on his face.

"Not a thing," Sam replied breezily.

"Could we have three iced teas, please?" Emma asked him.

"Coming right up!" the steward replied, as he disappeared back belowdecks.

"This," Sam purred, stretching her arms over her head, "is what Sam Bridges was born to do. Yes, indeed! Ah and double ah!" She snuggled into the air mattress underneath her.

"I think this is what *everyone* was born

to do," Carrie joked, as she lay on her own air mattress right next to Sam's, her voice carrying over the sound of the gently lapping waves.

"And this is what Emma was born *doing*!" Sam pronounced, looking over at Emma, who, just like Sam and Carrie, was languidly sunbathing on an air mattress.

"If that was a crack about my being rich, I am above such mundane concerns," Emma teased airily. She sighed with contentment and enjoyed the gentle ocean breeze that played over her.

The three girls were sunning themselves on the bow deck of the *Popes Afloat*, a forty-five-foot cabin cruiser that, at the moment, was anchored five or six hundred yards off the main beach of Sunset Island, the fabulous resort island at the outer reaches of Casco Bay off the coast of Maine.

"Now, would I ever tease you about being rich?" Sam asked Emma innocently.

"Oh, never," Emma replied sarcastically.

Emma was used to Sam getting on her case because she came from one of the richest families in America. Lately she had been able to joke with Sam about it more than she used to.

3

It took a while, though, Emma recalled. *It wasn't so easy at first.*

"Compared to the vast majority of the world, all three of us are rich," Carrie pointed out, her eyes closed to the bright sun.

Sam gave her a look. "You mean to tell me there are people forced to live on a tighter budget than *moi?*"

"Yes, Sam," Carrie teased in a grave voice. "It's actually true."

Sam turned over to sun her back. "Hey, can you imagine someone like Emma's mother living on the 'B' word?" Sam asked. "As in *budget?*"

"Not unless it had unlimited zeros in it," Emma admitted. "But it's not her fault, really. I mean, my mother has always been rich. She doesn't know anything else."

"And she isn't *like* anyone else, either, for that matter," Sam added.

Sam's right. No one would ever say Katerina please-call-me-Kat Cresswell is like anyone else's mother, Emma thought to herself. *That's for sure. For example, how many people's mothers leave their husbands for a twenty-five-year-old struggling artist and then get back together with their husbands after the divorce is final?*

"Hey," Carrie exclaimed, "don't rag on

Emma's mother. If it wasn't for her, we wouldn't be out here this morning. It's her mother's friends' yacht."

"It was nice of the Popes to offer to have the captain take us out for a morning," Emma said.

"Which means we'll stay friends with Emma for at least the rest of the day," Sam joked. "Right, Carrie?"

"Right!" Carrie affirmed. All three girls laughed.

The steward quickly proved he was as good as his word. He reappeared, holding a tray of three tall glasses of iced tea, and a dish of sliced-and-diced pineapple topped with fresh-cut strawberries. He put the tray down next to the girls and quietly disappeared again.

"Ah, yes," Sam observed, "this *is* the life!" She reached over and took a slice of pineapple, tossed it in the air, and caught it in her mouth.

"Don't get too used to it," Carrie suggested. "We're still just three au pairs who got the morning off."

"Don't remind me." Sam sighed, reaching for one of the iced teas. "Becky and Allie were impossible last night—big fight with Dan. You know how they're about to start this job as counselors-in-training at

Club Sunset—the new day camp—well, they wanted his charge card to go shopping for new clothes for their job, and he said no."

"Dan Jacobs actually said no to the twins?" Carrie asked incredulously.

"I know, it's shocking," Sam agreed, sipping her iced tea.

"But I mean, really, what kind of clothes do you need to be a camp counselor?" Carrie asked.

"New ones!" Sam replied.

Emma smiled. Sometimes it was just too amazing to her that she was friends with Sam and Carrie. And not just friends— best friends! She'd never had two best friends before, and certainly never had friends like Sam and Carrie before she came to Sunset Island.

As the morning sun warmed her carefully sunscreened skin, Emma closed her eyes and her thoughts drifted back to the remarkable circumstances that had brought her, Sam, and Carrie together.

First, we all decided that we wanted to work as au pairs for a summer—that wasn't so easy for me, because no one in my family could believe I actually wanted to spend a summer working, instead of traveling first class around Europe or Asia or

6

some such place, like my mother says a Cresswell should, Emma mused.

Then, we all met at the International Au Pair Convention in New York City. That was lucky. Then, we all got au pair jobs here on Sunset Island! That was even luckier. Me with the Hewitt family, Sam with Dan Jacobs and his twins, and Carrie with rock star Graham Perry Templeton and his family. And now, we're all back for our second summer in a row.

My mother sure wouldn't pick Sam and Carrie to be my friends, that's for sure, Emma ruminated. *Sam? Who grew up in Junction, Kansas, who dropped out of college to be a dancer at Disney World? And Carrie, with her politically liberal parents, from Teaneck, New Jersey? Friends with Emma Cresswell, of the Boston Cresswells, a French major at Goucher College just like all the other women in my mother's family?*

We're so different from each other . . . maybe that's what makes it so great. We even look totally different from each other. Sam calls me the Ice Princess because I'm petite and blonde and blue-eyed and I like to wear, well, classic clothes. Meanwhile, she's tall and slender and has all this amazing red hair and really knows how to put together great outfits. But Sam's jealous of

7

Carrie because Carrie is really curvy, and Carrie's so bright and such a talented photographer, why, she's already had photos published in—

"Yo, Emma, beam back down to earth!" Sam yelled.

Emma pulled herself out of her daydream, opened her eyes, and shook her head slightly.

"I was daydreaming," Emma admitted.

"I'll say," Sam agreed. "Was it about the babe who brought us the iced tea?"

"No," Emma said.

Sam's face darkened. "About Kurt?"

"No," Emma said more firmly. She made it clear from her tone of voice that the subject of Kurt was off-limits.

"We're gonna have to go back in pretty soon," Carrie observed, looking at her watch. "I'm supposed to take Chloe for a play date with May Spencer-Rumsey's niece at one o'clock."

"No problem," Sam said. "What time is it now? Eleven-thirty?"

Emma looked at her watch and nodded. "Eleven thirty-five."

Sam sat up and stretched, looking toward the beach. "Check out the mob scene." There were now people all over the beach, setting up umbrellas, blankets, volleyball nets, and the like. Sam reached for a small pair of binoculars conveniently stowed on a rack in the bow and began scanning the beach. Suddenly, the binoculars stopped moving, and Sam began fiddling with the focus knobs on it.

"Babe alert, hoo-boy, major babe alert," Sam sang out in the tones of a ship's captain sounding a "Mayday SOS" alarm. "Check this guy out!" She took the binoculars and held them out to Emma, who had propped herself up on her elbows for the moment.

Emma shook her head no, but Sam insisted, and finally Emma took them.

"Where?" she asked, sighing.

"Lifeguard chair to the left," Sam instructed her, "down toward the water, about thirty feet from the waterline, on a blue striped blanket, wearing the baggy red shorts."

Emma panned down from the lifeguard chair as Sam instructed, toward the water.

Okay, okay, she thought, as she focused on a well-built guy with startling, jet-black hair combed back in a sort of 1940s movie-star style, *he's cute.*

Carrie took the binoculars from Emma and zeroed in on the same guy. "Yep, very cute," she agreed. "Sam has some sort of guy radar."

"I wouldn't mind snuggling with him on a cold night under a warm blanket," Sam said, taking the binoculars back from Carrie and refocusing on the guy on the beach.

"Sam," Carrie began, "I thought you and Pres—"

"Hey," Sam defended herself. "I'm only looking. A girl can look, can't she?"

"Well, all I have to say is, it's a good thing you're on this boat and not on that beach," Carrie stated.

"I look at it this way," Sam mused. "My body is totally true to Pres, but my mind is a free-thinker."

Emma laughed and shook her head. Since the previous summer, Sam had been in an on-again/off-again relationship with Presley Travis, a totally gorgeous and incredibly cool guy from Tennessee, who played bass in the rock band Flirting With Danger—or, as everyone knew them, the Flirts. Emma and Sam were backup singer-dancers in the band, and Carrie's boyfriend was the band's lead singer, Billy Sampson.

It used to be so perfect, Emma thought with a sigh, *when we were all couples— Carrie and Billy, Sam and Pres, and me and Kurt. But then Sam and Pres broke up because of Sam's being such a big flirt, and then Kurt and I . . . no. I can't think about Kurt now. I won't. It just hurts too much. Well, at least Carrie and Billy are tighter than ever. And Sam and Pres are back together again.*

"Emma, oh Emma," Sam called, "you're getting that look in your eyes again!"

Emma pulled herself back to reality.

"I was thinking about the band," she said, telling a half-truth.

"Cool," Sam commented, "one of my favorite topics." She reached for another piece of pineapple and popped it into her mouth. "Can you believe that Diana is actually out of the band? I am so psyched!"

"I have to admit, it makes me pretty happy, too," Emma agreed with a grin.

They were referring to Diana De Witt, their archenemy, who until recently had been the third backup singer-dancer for the Flirts.

"So many scary changes," Carrie said softly, with a shudder.

Emma nodded solemnly. She knew that Carrie was thinking about the Flirts' drummer, Sly Smith, who had recently been diagnosed with full-blown AIDS. He'd been sick, but had rallied and had rejoined the band. Now, though, he was out again. Maybe forever.

"Any news about Sly?" Emma asked Carrie.

"Not a word," Carrie replied. "He's home in Maryland now, in the hospital with AIDS-related pneumonia—but then you guys already know that."

"We should write him another letter," Sam suggested.

"I wish we could do more," Emma said softly, "though I don't know what that would be."

They were all quiet for a moment, staring out at the beach, where healthy people frolicked in the sunshine, in sharp contrast to Sly fighting for his life in some hospital.

"So I guess the guys are still looking for another new drummer," Sam finally said.

"I guess," Emma agreed, hugging her knees to her chest.

"And a new backup singer," Carrie added.

"That part I'm thrilled about," Sam said. "No more Diana! Free at last! Free at last!"

"Well, you know I can't stand Diana, either, but she's a really good singer," Emma reminded Sam. "I don't think it's going to be so easy to replace her."

Carrie scratched a mosquito bite on her calf. "Wouldn't the guys consider just keeping Maia in the band?"

Maia was the singer who was temporarily taking Diana's place.

"They don't think she's good enough," Sam said with a shrug.

"Do you?" Carrie asked Sam.

She shrugged again. "I guess maybe there's someone better out there—she just better not be a redhead!"

Carrie laughed. "Why, Sam, can't you take the comp?"

Sam raised her eyebrows loftily. "I am merely thinking of the look of the band."

"How about a bald girl?" Emma suggested. "You know, a kind of Sinéad O'Connor look."

"I'll tell you who would be perfect," Sam mused. "How about a great singer and great dancer who Pres doesn't think is very cute. Now that I've got him back, I am not taking any chances!"

Carrie reached for the last piece of pineapple. "But Sam, what happened to that famous confidence of yours?"

Sam thought for a moment. "You're right. Let's go with bald. I would *definitely* feel confident around a bald girl!"

*   *   *

"Hey," Sam said, as she walked down the gangplank from the *Popes Afloat* after it had been tied up to one of the slips of the Sunset marina, "it looks like there's a welcoming party for us."

Emma looked to where Sam was pointing. Sam was right. Up the dock, sitting on one of the old wooden benches, dressed nearly identically in old jeans and T-shirts, were Presley Travis and Billy Sampson, deep in conversation. As the girls walked off the boat, even from this distance, Emma saw both guys' faces light up in broad smiles.

For Carrie and Sam, Emma thought with a pang. *Not for me. Kurt should be with them. No! Stop it, Emma! Just stop it!*

As Emma made her way down the gangplank to join her friends, Billy and Pres got up and approached them.

"My kind of greeting party," Sam commented, as she embraced Pres quickly. Billy also gave Carrie a quick hug and a kiss.

"We knew we could find you here, together," Billy explained. "I called the Templetons looking for you."

14

"So we were just talkin' some band business, enjoyin' the day, waitin' on you," Pres drawled in his sweet Tennessee accent.

"So, what's up?" Sam asked, pulling on an oversized man's T-shirt over her bikini.

"Auditions," Billy answered. "Tomorrow. Play Café. Two to four. Can you guys make it?"

Carrie shook her head. "Not a chance," she explained. "Claudia's got me helping her get the house ready for some party."

"How about you guys?" Billy asked Emma and Sam.

"No sweat," Sam said. "The monsters are working at Club Sunset all day. I just need to pick them up at five."

"I think I'm free," Emma said, trying to think ahead to her schedule for the next day. She knew she had to babysit for Katie Hewitt in the morning, and then for all the Hewitt kids that night, but she thought she had the afternoon off.

"Well, be there if you can," Pres advised. "We want to check the vocal blend, make sure it's right."

"What about a drummer?" Carrie asked. "Did you find someone?"

Billy nodded. "You'll meet him tomorrow afternoon. He's good. Really good."

"Jake Fisher is his name," Pres said. "He used to drum for Front Money down in D.C. before they broke up."

"They were awesome," Billy smiled.

"I hope he's sane," Carrie commented.

Everyone nodded in agreement. The last time the Flirts found a replacement for Sly, they'd hired a guy named Nick Trenton. Nick hadn't lasted long because the band discovered he'd stolen equipment from them. He was also a sleaze when it came to girls.

"He's sane," Billy assured them.

"Yeah," Sam said. "It's us who aren't. Why are we standing out here in the sun when we could be in the snack bar?"

"You got a point, girl," Pres said. "Maybe you'd like to be our drummer."

"No thanks, big guy," Sam replied. "But I'll let you buy me a Coke anyway. And some food. I'm starved."

"You must have some kind of hollow leg," Pres teased Sam. "Where do you put it?" He tickled her in the ribs and she shooed him off. Then, with their arms around each other, they headed for the snack bar.

Emma watched them, and a sad smile played over her lips. *Am I ever going to have that again?* she wondered, a lump in her throat. *Will I ever be able to fall back in love? Is my heart always going to hurt me? And if I could turn the clock back with Kurt, would I do the same thing all over again?*

Or did I make the biggest mistake I ever made in my life?

TWO

"Okay," Billy called to the small group of girls sitting in the Play Café waiting to audition for Diana's former backup spot, "let's listen up, please." He scanned a list of names on a clipboard. "Just call out 'Here,' when I say your name."

Emma glanced at the clock. Two o'clock sharp. There were about ten girls sitting haphazardly at some of the Play Café's otherwise empty tables. They'd all been sent out by their agents to audition for Diana's slot—evidently, Billy and Pres had put the word out carefully. Instead of placing an ad in the paper and having open auditions, as they had done in the past, this time they were only seeing girls who were far enough along to have a professional agent. Since the Flirts tried out a lot of their new material at the café and had played several gigs there, the owner of the place was letting the band hold their auditions there before the café opened for business at 5:00 P.M.

Sam, who was sitting to Emma's left, leaned over to her friend and whispered, "Glad we don't have to go through this again."

"That's for sure," Emma echoed.

"Yeah," Sam said, "but you didn't have to do it twice!"

Emma laughed quietly. Earlier in the summer, Sam had, in one of her characteristically impetuous moves, quit the band with the idea that she was going to go out on the road as part of a dance duo with a gorgeous dancer-friend named X. She'd quickly decided that the idea was a big fat mistake, but by then the band had made up its mind to replace her.

"I had to beg them to let me audition for my own spot!" Sam recalled.

"To know you is to love you." Emma grinned. "They let you."

"Can I help it if I'm irresistible?" Sam asked, scanning the girls waiting to audition. "Do you realize that if we weren't already in the band, we wouldn't even *be* at this audition, since we don't have an agent?"

Emma nodded thoughtfully. "Frankly, it intimidates me a lot."

"Me, too," Sam admitted in a rare burst of honesty.

"Okay, everyone is here, cool," Billy said when he'd finished calling out the names. Jay Bailey, the group's keyboard player, handed Billy a stack of pictures and resumés. "You guys were all sent here by agents or by references," he said, looking over the group of women, "and some of you we've seen already."

"He's talking about Kimber Avery," Sam whispered, glancing over at a very pretty blonde girl who was wearing a low-cut black tank dress. "I can't believe she'd audition again after being in the band for about five minutes."

"I noticed Maia isn't here," Emma whispered back.

"You'll be singing with our keyboard player, Jay," Billy continued, "and then we'll make the first cut. Then we'll do some harmony, then Sam and Emma over there will show you a dance combination, which you'll do, and then we'll decide. Any questions?"

"Hey, he never told us we were going to dance!" Sam exclaimed to Emma.

21

"Surprise, surprise," Emma whispered back.

"I'm Delaney Espinoza," said a petite Hispanic girl with spiky hair, who had on ripped jeans and a low-cut gauzy shirt. "I thought there were four guys in your band."

Billy's face darkened. "Our new drummer's coming in an hour," he explained. "We don't need him for this first part."

"Isn't Sly Smith your drummer?" Delaney asked.

"Not right now," Billy said in a rigid voice, "he's sick again."

Delaney shrugged. "Sorry to hear that, man."

"You used to sing with The Ravers, right?" Pres asked Delaney, deftly changing the subject.

She nodded. "We broke up when Seth died of a heroin overdose—well, I guess you read about it in the papers and everything. What a waste, huh?"

"Your band was great," Pres said. "I heard ya'll when you opened for Melissa Etheridge at the Bottom Line in New York."

"You want to go first?" Billy asked her.

Delaney shrugged. "Why not? Call me Laney, by the way."

Laney got up, walked confidently up on the stage, smiled at Jay, who was sitting behind his electric piano, and waited.

"Anything in particular you want to hear?" she asked Billy.

"Whatever appeals to you," Billy replied. "Give us sixteen bars or so, something up-tempo—we're looking for a big belt sound."

Laney leaned over and said a few words to Jay, who nodded easily.

"I'm gonna do the end of Linda Ronstadt's 'When Will I Be Loved'," Laney said, mentioning the name of an old country-rock classic.

Jay gave her a brief intro, and Laney launched into the song. Her voice was throaty with no vibrato.

I've never heard a sound quite like that before, Emma realized as she listened intently.

The song had a big range, and Laney finished with an astonishing gospel-sounding riff that left Sam and Emma shaking their heads in wonder.

"They might as well cancel the rest of the auditions—they've found her," Sam said to Emma. Emma nodded her head in agreement. She looked over at Billy and Pres, who both had broad smiles on their faces.

And these guys never let on what they're thinking in auditions, Emma marveled. *They're really excited by what they just heard, I know it.*

"How could I possibly sing with her?" Emma whispered nervously to Sam. "She'll blow me right off the stage!"

Then Emma snuck a glance at the other auditioners. Most of them sat there glumly, and one or two were actually packing up their sheet music as if to leave, including Kimber Avery.

I guess I'm going to be getting to know a girl named Laney, Emma thought. *She seems very self-confident and tough. And she's incredibly talented.*

Billy called the names of all the other girls, who basically went through the motions of singing. They were actually really good, but not anywhere in Laney's class. Emma glanced over at the Hispanic girl. She'd reassumed her seat and had taken out a copy of *Rock On* magazine to read. She was the epitome of cool.

"Erin Kane?" Billy asked, when there was only one auditioner left who hadn't yet sung.

Emma saw a big girl with wild long blond hair—even wilder and longer than Sam's red hair—look up and smile.

"That's me," Erin answered.

"You're up," Billy told her.

"So I am," Erin said, a grin spreading across her face. She picked up her sheet music and started walking toward the stage.

"She's cute," Emma whispered to Sam, "in her own way."

"No way," Sam disagreed, "she's fat."

"Yeah," Emma said, not disputing what Sam had said, "but she looks great anyway."

Erin was overweight—Emma guessed probably a size eighteen or twenty—but she was very pretty, with that wild long blond hair, high cheekbones, perfect subtle makeup with bright red matte lipstick, and very cute legs. She had on black cowboy boots, black tights, a short black miniskirt, a black T-shirt, and a black-and-white checkered blazer jacket with strategically placed rhinestones that glistened under the Play Café's stage lights.

Erin took her place at the microphone next to Jay's piano. She still had the same confident grin on her face. Emma took a glance over at Laney. Laney's head was still buried in the magazine.

"So you're Erin Kane," Billy remarked.

"I sure hope so," the girl replied easily,

"or else I'm having a really, really bad day."

Everyone cracked up at Erin's joke, Sam and Emma included.

"Graham Perry recommended you, huh?" Billy said, checking his list.

"It sounds more impressive than it probably is," Erin said with a smile. "I just filled in for one of his backups when she came down with the mumps."

"So, do you dance, too?" Billy asked her.

"Jazz, some tap," Erin replied. "But I really hope you're not thinking about adding a tap number to your set."

"We're not," Billy assured her with a grin. "You ready to sing?"

"Sure," Erin answered. She turned to Jay and said something, Jay played one lone chord and Erin launched into Graham Perry's classic "I Rock for Love."

She's good, Emma thought to herself, as she listened. *Correction. She's great! Her voice is totally different from Laney's. It's really strong, but kind of sweet and pure.* Emma glanced at Laney, who was looking up for the first time. *Huh,* Emma thought. *She knows her competition when she hears it, I'll bet.*

"Thanks, Erin," Billy said, a grin spreading on his face again as Erin finished her song. "Just have a seat."

"Wow, what a voice," Emma whispered to Sam as she watched Billy turn to confer quickly with Jay and Pres.

"Yeah, great voice," Sam agreed, "but she's too big. The guys will never go for that."

"Oh, come on," Emma said, "they wouldn't eliminate someone that good because she's overweight!"

"Wanna bet?" Sam asked in a jaded voice. "Just watch."

The three guys huddled by Jay's piano for a couple of minutes, and then apparently reached some kind of an agreement.

"Okay, we want to thank you all for auditioning," Billy said, walking to the edge of the stage. "Laney Espinoza and Erin Kane, please stay. The rest of you can go. And thanks again. We really appreciate it."

The other girls gathered up their stuff and walked, somewhat dejectedly, toward the door.

"Erin's still in the running—you were wrong," Emma told Sam.

"So far," Sam agreed. "But Laney's gonna get it."

"What we're gonna do now is check your vocal blends with our two current backups."

"That's us!" Sam called out, waving at Laney and Erin.

Laney nodded at them curtly; Erin smiled warmly.

"We're gonna go over the harmonies on 'Love Junkie'—you guys know the tune?"

"I've heard the Flirts sing it a few times," Laney said. "No problem."

"Well, I'd like to say I know it," Erin began, "but I haven't ever heard your band. I just moved to this area from Seattle."

"Can you read music?" Billy asked her.

"Sure," Erin said. Billy handed her a sheet and she studied it carefully.

"Where's Jake?" Billy asked, turning back to Pres. "He said he'd be here at three."

"Right here!" said a male voice from the door of the Play Café.

Emma and Sam followed the sound of the voice. A rangy, muscular guy with straight black hair combed off his face strode into the club. He was wearing a blue T-shirt with jeans and he had some kind of crystal around his neck on a string.

"Hey, Jake," Billy called to him.

"Hey, Billy," he called back.

"Emma, Sam, this is Jake Fisher, our new drummer," Billy remarked, reaching out and shaking Jake's hand.

He looks familiar to me, Emma thought, as she reached over and shook Jake's hand herself. She sensed that Sam had the same feeling.

After Jake went up on the stage, Emma turned to Sam. Sam had the strangest grin on her face.

"Do you feel like you've seen him someplace before?" Sam asked.

"Yes," Emma answered, "but I don't know—"

"I know," Sam said triumphantly.

"You do?"

"Sure," Sam responded.

"Where?" Emma asked.

"Guess," Sam prompted her.

"Oh come on, Sam," Emma nudged her friend.

"I'll help you," Sam said conspiratorially. "You know the guy we were scoping out yesterday with the binoculars?"

"Oh God, you're right—"

"Yup," Sam said, "that's him." She looked over at Jake again and rubbed her hands together eagerly. "Who needs binoculars, anyway? He's even more buff in person!"

"Well, they're both great singers, they can both move—these are two talented girls," Jay said, as the members of the band gathered around one of the Play Café's tables. They had just finished the audition, and Laney and Erin had left the club a few minutes earlier.

"I agree," Jake said in his husky voice. "They're both really good."

Now, it was decision time.

"What do you think, Pres?" Billy asked his best buddy.

"Well, it's a close call," Pres mused.

"Go for it," Billy prompted him.

"Erin's got a better blend—Laney is used to singing lead and her voice is really distinctive. On the other hand, we can probably work on her blend, and Laney's got a better look," Pres explained.

"That's a matter of opinion, man," Jake spoke up. "I think they're both attractive, and they'd both look fine on stage."

"Erin is kind of, well, fat," Sam pointed out.

"She's not thin," Billy agreed, "but she's really pretty."

"I don't know," Jay mused. "I mean, maybe she's too big to fit in."

Billy raised his eyebrows at Jay. "You believe that?"

Jay thought about it a minute. "Nah. And I agree with Pres about the blend." He looked at Pres. "Laney sang a lot of lead with The Ravers, didn't she?"

Pres nodded. "But that doesn't mean we shouldn't give her a shot."

"She's great, no doubt about it," Billy said. "But I don't know about her singing backup. I mean, she'd need to hold back. The idea is to make the band sound great, not to call attention to herself. Could she do that?"

"Maybe," Jake said. "But you know for sure Erin could. I thought her blend with Emma and Sam was really great."

Billy tapped a pencil on the table pensively. "I did, too," he agreed. "So, what do we know about this girl, other than that she once filled in for one of Graham's backup singers?"

Jay Bailey reached for the piles of pictures and resumés and began flipping through them, looking for Erin Kane's. He flipped to her bio sheet.

"Here it is," Jay said. "Says she's a performing arts major at Emerson College in Boston, eighteen years old, family just moved to the East Coast and is living in a summer house on the island. She's been singing semiprofessionally for two years with various bands. Here's what she wrote— 'Hobbies: singing, singing, and singing.'"

"She has a sense of humor," Billy commented with a smile.

"I thought she was very funny," Emma added.

"I think we've made our decision," Billy said, getting up. "Anyone disagree?"

No one did.

"Cool," Billy added. "I'll go call her now."

Emma turned to Sam, and the two of them grinned at one another.

"Wow, we have a new bandmate!" Emma said to Sam.

Sam nodded. "You think we're going to like her?"

"She seemed really nice," Emma replied, pushing her blond hair behind one ear. "And she's an incredibly great singer."

"Yeah," Sam agreed. "And no matter how much I ever eat, I'll look thin next to her!"

Emma laughed. "You are hopeless, Sam."

Emma gathered up her things and headed toward the door, feeling really hopeful about Erin joining the band. *Somehow, I know it's going to be a lot more fun being in this band with Erin,* Emma thought, *than it was being in this band with Diana!*

THREE

"There she is!" Sam cried to Carrie and Emma, waving her arms wildly, paying no attention to the fact that she nearly delivered a karate chop to several innocent bystanders. "Hey, Erin, over here!" Sam then stood up by the girls' usual booth in the Play Café and continued to try to get Erin Kane's attention, competing with the noise of the packed café.

It was the next evening, and Emma, Sam, and Carrie had arranged to meet the new Flirts' backup there "just to scope her out," as Sam had put it. Sam had gotten Erin's number from Billy and called to invite her, and the new girl had readily agreed.

"Erin!" Sam cried again, as Erin looked uncertainly around the Play Café.

"Try the whistle you learned from Darcy," Emma suggested.

Sam put two fingers between her teeth and whistled loudly.

Carrie winced. "That is a sound only dogs should hear."

"Hey, it worked, didn't it?" Sam pointed out, as Erin noticed her and began to make her way through the crowd.

Emma noticed again how pretty Erin was, with her heart-shaped face, wild hair, and very definite sense of style. Tonight she had on jeans, combat boots and a gauzy baby-doll top over a camisole. *And it looks really cute on her,* Emma realized. *She's large, but she's curvy, and I bet lots of guys would think she's really sexy, too.*

Emma looked over at her friends and had to smile at their different styles. Carrie had on jeans and a Yale sweatshirt, Sam had on a vintage black velvet and lace dress from a thrift store, with black fishnet hose and her trademark red cowboy boots. She looked down at her own outfit—a short white skirt and a white summer sweater with tiny pearl buttons that bared the bottom of her tanned stomach—then she looked back over at Erin again. *I guess all four of us have different styles,* she thought.

"Too bad she doesn't take off a few

pounds," Sam said, as she watched Erin stop to chat with someone.

"Stop that," Emma scolded, "you'll hurt her feelings!"

"Hi!" Erin said when she finally reached their table. "This place is hopping!"

"Yeah, it always is," Sam agreed, moving over so Erin could slide into the booth next to her. "You already know Emma, and this is Carrie Alden."

Erin stuck out her hand to Carrie across the table. "Great to meet you," she said with a smile. "Do you sing, too?"

Carrie laughed. "Not really," she said.

"Yes, really," Emma corrected her. "Carrie sang with the Flirts on the road for a while."

"Oh, yeah?" Erin asked. "So why didn't you audition yesterday?"

"Because I would have made an idiot out of myself," Carrie replied with a laugh. "I filled in when Diana was injured in the fire—but only because it was an emergency. Trust me, from what I hear, you sing rings around me."

Erin grinned and ran her hand through her wild curls. "Well, it's my favorite thing in the world to do."

"Mine's photography," Carrie said.

"Oh, sure," Sam snorted. "Your favorite

thing to do is to swap saliva with Billy." She looked over at Erin. "Billy Sampson is her guy."

"He seems great," Erin said. "Very talented guy."

"Whoa, four babes, one table, I'm in heaven!" a drunk guy bellowed as he reeled up to their table.

"This place is a zoo," Erin commented.

"I want to suck face with all of you!" he yelled at them, throwing his arms wide and practically falling over.

"Yeah, and he's definitely one of the animals," Sam said. She looked at the guy. "Here's a subtle tip. Die."

"Ooooh, nasty," the guy said, wagging his finger at Sam. Then he got lost again in the throngs of people.

Emma looked around the room. It seemed even more crowded than usual. A rowdy crowd of guys had just come in and they all looked pretty looped, a hot dart game was in progress in one corner, and the two video games were surrounded by people waiting to play.

"Haven't you been here before?" Sam asked Erin. "I thought everyone between the ages of eighteen and twenty-five basically *lived* here."

"Well, I've only been on the island a

couple of weeks, actually. It's a great place."

"We hang out here a lot," Carrie said.

"With the exception of a couple of drunk morons, this place is really hip," Erin said with a laugh. "Listen, I have to tell you that I am so excited about singing with the Flirts. I stopped by their house earlier today and picked up the demo tape you guys did, and I was just totally blown away!"

"Yeah, we are pretty terrif," Sam agreed happily. She craned her neck. "Didn't we order about ten hours ago? I'm dying of hunger, here."

"Me, too," Erin said. "I didn't have time to eat dinner. What did you order?"

"A super-deluxe pizza," Carrie replied. "Okay with you?"

"We can get you some cottage cheese or something, if you want," Sam said.

Emma winced and kicked Sam under the table.

Erin smiled. "I'm not really big on cottage cheese. The pizza sounds great, as long as there's iced tea to go with it."

Emma pushed a glass toward her. "A girl after our own heart. This one is yours—we already ordered it."

"Great," Erin said. She looked around the room. "Wild! Truly wild!"

"Hey, Big Stuff!" The same drunk guy reeled back over to the girls' table. "Blondie!" he added, stopping in front of Erin.

She raised her eyebrows at him and didn't say a word.

"The bigger the cushion the better the pushin', know what I mean?" He leered at her.

"Gosh, did you think that up all by yourself?" Erin asked him with feigned innocence.

He belched. "Yeah," he said with pride. "Wanna go out to the parking lot and get naked, Tubs?"

Without saying a word, Erin picked up her glass of iced tea. Then she held out the elastic waistband on the guy's shorts and calmly poured her tea into his pants.

"Yeow!" he screeched. He jumped backward, stumbled, and fell into a group of his friends, who were all laughing at him hysterically.

"I guess she ranked you, Barry!" one guy yelled.

"Wet your pants much?" another one said. They all cracked up and carried the wet drunk out the front door of the café.

"That was priceless!" Sam cried. "I am truly impressed."

"I have to tell you," Erin said happily, "that was so much fun!"

Emma laughed. *I really like this girl,* Emma thought, the grin still on her face. *I think she's incredibly funny, nice, and really pretty. Of course, my mother would think she should run off to some fat farm, or go on a liquid diet. But who cares what narrow-minded people like my mother think, anyway?*

"So," Erin said, reaching for the tall pepper shaker on the table and raising it to her lips in imitation of a microphone being held by a TV talk show host, "why don't you tell our studio audience how you three incredible vixens met?"

Sam looked at Emma. "You noticed how she noticed how incredible we are—she's very observant."

"You would say that," Emma replied.

"Miss Emma Cresswell, blond backup singer for the band Flirting With Danger," Erin continued in her announcer's voice, "thank you for volunteering." Erin pushed the pepper shaker over in Emma's face.

"Go on, Emma," Carrie prompted, "tell her."

Just at that instant the pizza arrived,

and all four girls dug in happily. But Erin continued to prompt Emma, and finally Emma told her the story of how they'd all met, along with some background on each of them and their families.

"So what about you?" Sam asked Erin, as she reached for another slice of pizza.

"What about me?" Erin answered innocently.

"What's your story, babe? And don't leave out any dirt, because I live for it," Sam instructed.

Erin looked over at Carrie. "Is she always like this?"

"Usually she's worse," Carrie said mildly, sipping her tea.

"Well, it's not a pretty story," Erin began solemnly. "My parents were missionaries who gambled away their life savings in Vegas, at which point I was forced into a life of crime and topless dancing."

Sam eyed Erin. "And may I point out that you have a lot of top to dance."

Erin cracked up. "You slay me!" She reached for another slice of pizza. "Actually, it's not a very interesting story."

"Okay, so you're a great singer with a boring life," Sam stated. "What I want to know is where you got that great hair from."

"A bottle named Clairol," Erin joked. "No, I think I inherited it from my father."

"He must have great hair," Emma commented, reaching for the iced tea pitcher.

"Actually, he's bald," Erin said honestly, then she laughed. "But he used to have great hair!"

"So, what's he do? For a living, I mean," Sam asked, licking some tomato sauce off her pinkie.

Erin got a funny look on her face.

What's that all about? Emma asked herself. Sam didn't ask anything really prying.

Erin sighed and took another bite of pizza. "I'm sorry, it's no big thing, really," she said. She put the pizza down. "He basically lost his job a couple of weeks ago."

"You're kidding," Carrie said.

"Nope," Erin replied. "The economy sucks, and my dad got 'riffed.'"

"What's that mean?" Sam asked, totally baffled.

"It means 'reduction in forces,'" Erin explained, "and it's corporate-speak for when a big company decides they have too many employees and that they need to fire a whole bunch of them at once."

"That's terrible," Carrie empathized.

"Who did your dad work for?" Emma asked. "What did he do?"

"He worked for Mach Five Limited, the cosmetics company," Erin replied. "Ever hear of it?"

"Yeah, sure," Carrie said, "they're this really huge company, right?"

"Not as huge as they were five weeks ago," Erin pointed out ruefully. "They let a thousand people go. My dad was one of them."

"What does your mother do?" Carrie asked.

"She's your basic housewife," Erin replied, then she made a face. "I hate that term, don't you? I mean, it sounds like she's the wife of a house. What I mean is, she's never worked outside our home, so it's really rough that my dad got laid off."

"What does your dad do?" Emma asked again. She dabbed her lips with her napkin.

"He worked in the perfume department," Erin explained. "He's a nose."

Sam swallowed her iced tea with a gulp. "Say what?"

"A nose," Erin repeated. "It's an industry term for the person who mixes the ingredients and makes up perfumes. He's a nose."

"Wow," Sam commented. "You mean he designs perfume? Cool!"

"Designed," Erin corrected Sam with a sigh. "It's past tense now."

"So, did your dad ever sniff out any famous perfumes?" Sam asked.

"Ever hear of StarStruck?"

"No," Sam cried, "get out of town! I wear that one sometimes! I used to have a boyfriend who wanted me to practically *bathe* in the stuff!"

"My dad created it," Erin said simply.

"Now that's some seriously cool beans," Sam marveled, using an expression she'd picked up from Pres.

"Yeah, I've always been really proud of him," Erin agreed. "Only now he's not creating anything. It doesn't seem right, does it?"

"No, it really doesn't," Carrie agreed quietly.

"Anyway, I'm kind of hoping that singing with the Flirts will help me make some money for college," Erin explained, idly stirring the ice in her tea. "My parents won't be able to afford my tuition in the fall without my helping out."

The girls were all quiet for a moment.

I can't imagine what that's like, Emma thought. *No one in my family has ever had to worry about a job or about money. I am so incredibly lucky. . . .*

"How long did he work there?" Carrie finally asked.

"Oh, not long," Erin said.

So that explains it, Emma thought. *He must have been just recently hired. . . .*

"Only twenty-three years," Erin added bitterly.

"That really sucks," Sam said in a low voice.

"My feelings exactly," Erin agreed.

"So, what's he going to do?" Emma asked with concern.

"Look for a job," Erin said simply. "I mean, they really screwed him. First they transferred him from the Seattle plant to the new plant in Portland, then after we picked up our lives and moved, they laid him off. Right now we're staying at my uncle and aunt's house here on the island. I don't know what's going to happen."

"Can he find another job?" Sam asked.

"He'll try," Erin replied with a shrug. "But there aren't a lot of positions available for a nose, and perfume is basically my dad's life."

Everyone grew quiet again.

"Oh, please, I did not intend this to turn into a pity party for one!" Erin cried. She shook her long curls back over her shoulders. "Let's talk about something else! Something interesting, like . . . guys!"

"My favorite topic," Sam cheered. "Did you know that Pres is my one and only?"

"Lucky you," Erin said. "He's such a cutie, and his accent is to die for!"

"Do you have a boyfriend?" Carrie asked Erin.

"Nope," Erin said. "I was in this long relationship back in Seattle. But I had to end it. I mean, here I thought I really loved this guy, and then I found out he was sleeping with my best friend at the same time he was sleeping with me."

"That is the lowest thing I ever heard!" Sam cried.

"And your best friend wasn't much of a best friend," Carrie added.

"Tell me about it," Erin agreed. "Well, live and learn, I say. Anyhow, now I'm free and I'm looking!"

Well, she's not a virgin, Emma thought to herself. *And I really admire her confidence . . . her whole attitude. This is one cool person.*

"Stick with me," Sam said. "I know every hot guy on this island. In fact—"

"Well, well, well, what have we here?

The three ugly step-sisters have a new buddy!" came a nasty female voice.

Emma closed her eyes and sighed. *I'd know that voice anywhere,* she realized. *Diana De Witt, the girl we all love to hate. She's always hated me, ever since we went to boarding school together in Switzerland, and now she hates Carrie and Sam, too. She's the most evil girl I've ever met in my life.*

"Hello, Diana," Emma said in a frosty voice. "Good-bye, Diana."

"Now, now," Diana chided Emma. "You could at least comment on my new outfit."

Emma looked over at Diana, who had on an aqua bra top that matched her aqua eyes, with wide-legged aqua pants that fell in perfect creases to the floor. Her chestnut curls fell sexily into her eyes, and as usual, she looked incredible.

"Lovely outfit," Emma said in a flat voice. "Now go away."

"Why, Emma," Diana said, her voice full of false sweetness, "you used to be so well-bred at boarding school. You know, hanging out with trash has really lowered your standards of behavior."

Erin gave Diana a look. "Who are you?" she asked with distaste.

"Funny, I was just going to ask you the same thing," Diana said, looking Erin over from head to toe. "After all, I have to wait for my date, so I wouldn't mind being amused for a few minutes."

Erin reached over with her hand. "I'm Erin Kane," she said directly. "And you're?"

"Erin Kane!" Diana said, ignoring Erin's extended hand, her voice full of false surprise. "I've heard of you! Aren't you the new backup singer for Flirting With Danger?"

"That's right," Erin said. "I'm—"

"Well, well, well, congratulations!" Diana said, realizing that Erin had no idea who she was.

"Diana, maybe you'd better leave," Carrie suggested in a low voice.

"Are you kidding?" Diana asked. "It's such a pleasure to meet . . . my replacement!"

"Ah, the pieces are beginning to fall into place," Erin said, nodding.

"My, my, aren't you quick," Diana commented. She looked Erin up and down again. "This is the best the Flirts could do? Please."

"Diana used to sing backup for the Flirts," Emma said quietly to Erin.

Erin's smile never flagged. "I gathered that," she said.

"You know, I feel so much better, now that I've actually met you!" Diana said gaily.

"Look, Diana, get out of here—" Carrie began.

Diana ignored her. "But you know, I do feel bad for the band. I mean, you guys are going to have to change the name of the band to Flirting With Disaster!"

"She's a better singer than you'll ever be, Diana," Sam spat.

"I don't care if she's a better singer than Mariah Carey," Diana shot back, "the stage still has to *support* her!"

Sam jumped up, glaring at Diana.

"Or maybe they could just change the name of the band to Flirting With a Diet!" Diana continued, on a roll. She looked at Erin. "But then, apparently you don't bother with things like diets do you, or you wouldn't be such a blimp!"

"Either you walk away or I make you walk away," Sam hissed at Diana.

"Sit down, Sam," Carrie said, pulling on Sam's sleeve.

Emma looked at Erin to see how she was taking all this abuse about her weight. There was steel in Erin's eyes, true, but

Emma could see that Diana's words also hurt.

Of course they hurt! Emma thought. *They'd hurt anyone. And she is overweight. Not that it matters. Does it?*

"I'm not sitting down," Sam stated, standing practically nose-to-nose with Diana. "She deserves to get her butt kicked, and it would give me great satisfaction."

"Don't do it on my account," Erin said, finally speaking up. She looked at Diana coolly. "It was a real pleasure to meet you, although I do have to add that I don't know how you face yourself in the mirror every morning," she added. "Too bad the guys kicked you out of the band, huh? You must have really pissed them off. I wonder how?"

Diana laughed. "No problem, honey," she said. "Have another cookie. Oh! There's my date!"

Diana had caught sight of a guy coming into the café out of the corner of her eye, and she flitted away from the girls to go join him. The girls' eyes followed her.

Diana went up to him and planted a warm, sensuous-looking kiss right on his lips. He was muscular and had wonderful dark hair combed straight back. Then she slung her arm through his and led him into the café.

Diana's date for the evening was none other than Jake Fisher, the Flirts' new drummer.

FOUR

"Can you believe she pulled that crap?" Sam bellowed into the phone. "I'd really like to maim her. Correction, I'd like to kill her! Slowly. But also painfully!"

"Maybe killing Diana is a little extreme," Emma replied, taking the portable phone out of the Hewitts' kitchen and wandering into the hallway. "But I know how you feel. Hold on a minute, okay?"

"Okay."

Emma turned back to the kitchen to Ethan and Wills Hewitt, who had just finished their breakfast. It was the next morning, and Sam had called Emma to see what her plans were for the day.

"Could you guys please go get ready for camp?" Emma asked the two boys. "We're leaving in a half hour."

"How come Ethan gets to be a counselor

and I have to be a stupid camper?" Wills whined.

"Because you *are* a stupid camper," Ethan answered his little brother.

"Ethan, please don't start," Emma warned gently.

"Yeah, okay," Ethan agreed, and he ran upstairs to get dressed.

"I'm back," Emma reported. "You know, it's amazing how well Ethan is doing as a counselor-in-training at Club Sunset. I mean, he's really growing up—he even teases Wills less often."

"Thank you for that progress report on the kiddies," Sam said dryly. "Now can we talk about something really important? Like Diana? Can you believe how mean she was to Erin last night?"

"She can be incredibly ugly," Emma agreed.

"God, she's just as lame," Sam ranted. "She loves to pick on people wherever they're the most insecure—ever notice that?"

"Yep," Emma agreed.

"I guess Erin must be used to people saying mean things about her weight," Sam added.

"That doesn't mean it didn't hurt her feelings," Emma pointed out.

"So, why doesn't she just lose weight, then?" Sam asked.

Emma sat down at the kitchen table. "Sam, I hate to point this out to you, but do you realize that with as much as you eat, if you had a different metabolism you'd weigh two hundred pounds?"

"Maybe," Sam agreed, "but if I did I would starve before I'd let myself get fat. You know who I'd like to see wake up fat? Diana. She'd probably kill herself, which would save me the trouble. Hey, can you believe she's actually going out with Jake?"

"One date," Emma pointed out. She got up and began to clear the breakfast dishes off the table.

"One date with Diana is one too many," Sam snorted. "I thought he was a nice guy."

"Just because he had a date with Diana doesn't mean he isn't a nice guy," Emma responded as she stuck the pitcher of juice into the refrigerator.

"Sure it does," Sam countered. "It means he's effectively brain damaged."

"Or his brain is located somewhere below his waist," Emma added.

Sam laughed. "You know, you are not the same vestal virgin I used to know. You just cracked a dirty joke!"

"So now I'm a dirty-joke-cracking vestal

virgin," Emma replied, going to the sink for a sponge to wipe off the table.

"Emma, I just had a terrible thought," Sam said in a serious tone. "Do you realize if you and I were in a plane crash tomorrow, we would die without knowing what it's like to do it?"

"Sam, we're not even going on a plane trip tomorrow," Emma pointed out as she wiped the table.

"Don't be so literal," Sam said. "I think you catch my drift."

An image snapped into Emma's mind of her and Kurt on the beach, wrapped in each other's arms. *I loved him and I wanted him so much,* she remembered sadly. *Even though I'm really attracted to Adam, it isn't the same. What if I never, ever feel that way again?*

". . . so then I'll do it with Pres," Sam concluded.

"What?" Emma asked, since she'd only heard the end of what Sam had just said.

"I said that if Pres and I keep on the way we are, I think I'll do it with him," Sam repeated. "Try to keep up with the conversation, huh?"

"I noticed Erin mentioned she isn't a virgin," Emma said, as she threw the sponge into the sink.

"Emma, hasn't it dawned on you that we are the last two living virgins in the entire United States?" Sam queried.

"Good," Emma said with a laugh. "I like being unique."

"Well, I feel like a freak sometimes," Sam said. "Hey, do you think it's okay if we suggest to Erin that she go on a diet? You know, as a friend."

Wait a second, Emma thought. *What is Sam saying? She just went through this whole thing about how mean Diana was to Erin, and now she's talking about suggesting to Erin that she should go on a diet!*

"Why would we want to do that?" Emma asked. "I think she looks fine the way she is."

"Emma, she's fat," Sam said bluntly.

"Beauty comes in all sizes and shapes," Emma replied.

"Yeah, right," Sam snorted. "That's real politically correct of you and everything, but gimme a major break!"

"I happen to mean it," Emma said firmly.

"Okay, let's talk professionally, then," Sam said. "I mean, it wouldn't matter if we weren't all singing together, but you gotta admit she'd look better on stage if she dropped like thirty or forty bills. And what kind of unis are we supposed to wear? You know we're gonna have to get all new outfits."

Emma sat back down at the kitchen table. "So, we'll find new outfits that look good on all three of us," she said. "I really do think she looks fine the way she is. If she's okay with it, I'm okay with it."

"But if she'd just lose, like thirty or forty pounds, we could wear the outfits we have!" Sam exclaimed. "I mean, they're so cute!"

I don't think Sam has any idea what it takes to lose thirty or forty pounds. But then, neither do I, Emma realized. "Look, Sam," she finally said, "I don't think we should say a thing, and I don't think we should put any pressure on Erin. The guys hired her, which means they're okay with how she looks, so let's just drop it."

"But how tough can it be to lose some weight?" Sam asked impatiently.

"Ask Carrie," Emma suggested. "Remember when she got so anxious about her weight during her freshman year at Yale that she became bulimic?"

"Yeah, I guess I do," Sam admitted.

"Sam! We've got to get to work!" Emma heard one of the twins yell.

"I've got to drive the monsters to camp," Sam said into the phone.

Wills and Ethan came careening down the stairs into the kitchen, hitting each other in the triceps with their knuckles.

"Stop that, please," Emma told them sternly. "I have to get going, too," Emma told Sam. "I'm going to hang out at the pool with Katie for awhile, so maybe I'll see you there."

"Okay," Sam agreed. "Later!"

Emma hung up. "Ready to go?" she asked the boys.

"How about letting me drive?" asked twelve-year-old Ethan.

"How about you could get arrested," Emma countered, picking up the car keys from the stand in the hall.

"He thinks he's so big," seven-year-old Wills taunted.

"That's right," Ethan said smugly. "And I'll always be bigger than you."

They were hitting each other in the triceps again as Emma headed out to the car.

Later that day, Emma and Carrie walked into the Cheap Boutique together.

"Remind me," Carrie said, "I've got to be back home in an hour."

"So do I," Emma replied. "I'm making dinner tonight."

"Me too," Carrie admitted.

"Lucky you," Emma said drolly.

"No, lucky you," Carrie countered, grinning.

As per usual, loud rock music pounded through the Cheap Boutique's doors out onto the street. The store was located right on Main Street in what passed for Sunset Island's downtown. It was in the middle of a block filled with cheap and not-so-cheap eateries, clothing stores, jewelry stores, and the like.

I've spent a lot of time in this store, Emma recalled. *How can I forget that day right after I first came to the island when I spent nearly a thousand dollars in here? And who ridiculed me about it? Diana De Witt. I hope that she's not inside shopping right now! She'd probably say nasty things about Kurt. Kurt. God, he actually slept with her last summer.* Emma got a sick feeling in her stomach.

"You think Diana's in here shopping?" Emma asked, as she and Carrie pushed their way through the double doors.

"What?" Carrie asked her. "Why would she be here?"

"Oh, I don't know," Emma said lightly, taking a quick look around inside. While the boutique was fairly crowded, Diana, thankfully, was nowhere in sight.

"What are you looking to buy?" Carrie asked her friend. It was so busy in the boutique that all the salespeople were busy—no one rushed over to help the girls.

"Oh, I don't know," Emma said, walking over to the counter of cosmetics and perfumes. "Maybe some perfume or something like that."

"What's that great stuff you usually wear?" Carrie asked.

"Some signature fragrance my mother's friend has made in Paris," Emma replied, idly looking at the cosmetics on the counter.

"Figures you'd wear custom-made perfume," Carrie joshed at her friend.

"Well, I'm getting kind of tired of it," Emma admitted. "Besides, Kat wears it, too, and I don't think I should smell like my mother."

"I agree," Carrie said, lifting a sample bottle of perfume and sniffing it. "Yuck, this stuff reeks of gardenias. So, how much does it cost Kat to get your stuff made up special?" Carrie wondered.

"I don't know," Emma answered honestly. "A lot. I never asked." She lightly sprayed a perfume on her wrist and sniffed it.

"I hardly ever wear perfume," Carrie commented, leaning against the counter. "Too fake or something."

"There's nothing you like?" Emma asked. "Ever?"

Carrie shrugged. "I don't know. I guess it's the same reason why I don't wear makeup. It just doesn't seem like me." She looked idly at the perfumes on the counter. "Hey, there's StarStruck, the one that Erin's father invented!"

Emma sniffed the stopper on the perfume. "Wasn't that a terrible story about her dad and his job?"

"Truly awful," Carrie agreed. She picked up a boxed perfume that was sealed in plastic. "Hey, you know what I really hate?"

"What?" Emma asked, sniffing another perfume.

"How they package all this stuff," Carrie pointed out. "Everything comes in a box, and all you do with the box is throw it away right after you open it."

"I think the box is supposed to make you want to buy the stuff more," Emma commented.

"It makes me want to buy it less," Carrie maintained. "What a waste! I mean, why don't we just go cut down a bunch of extra trees for nothing!"

"But you don't buy perfume anyway," Emma pointed out.

"Well, if I did," Carrie maintained, "I wouldn't buy one that came with a ton of packaging."

"You've got a point," Emma said.

A very rock-and-roll–looking salesperson with spiky blond hair, wearing a black leather motorcycle jacket and a black mini-skirt with holes in it, came over to wait on the girls.

"I know you," she said to Emma accusingly.

Oh God, Emma thought. *It's Diana De Witt's cousin, dressed in black leather.*

Emma was polite as always. "Do you?"

"Yeah," the salesgirl said. "You're somebody-or-other Cresswell."

"Emma," Emma filled in. "And you're?"

"Call me Rage. I only use one name," the girl said. "I'm a performance artist."

"An angry one, huh?" Carrie asked, biting her lip to keep from laughing.

"Look there's a lot in this world to be angry about," Rage snapped. "Like the ozone layer, and the rain forest, and the

61

fact that someone as talented as I am is forced to work in this stupid store just to make money to live. So what do you want?"

"How did you know who I was?" Emma asked with curiosity.

"Your picture's up in the back," Rage said blankly. "You won that trip."

Emma laughed. *God, I must be getting paranoid. She's right—my picture probably is up in the back room. I won that trip to Paradise Island through a contest they had here. There's every reason my picture would be up on a bulletin board!*

"So, look, you wanna buy something or not?" Rage asked as she bit off the nail on her pinky finger.

I hope she's a better performance artist than she is a salesperson, Emma thought. *She's got all the charm and people skills of an escaped convict.*

"No," Emma said coolly. "I was, but I'm not interested anymore."

"But Emma," Carrie said, "I thought you wanted—"

"I've changed my mind," Emma said. "Come on, we've got to get back to work." She took Carrie by the arm and started leading her to the door.

"Well, thanks for wasting my time!"

Rage yelled after them. "I can really make a commission on people like you!"

Carrie and Emma cracked up when they reached the street. "Where do they find people like that?" Carrie wondered.

"I don't know, but I wasn't about to buy perfume from her!" Emma said with a laugh.

"You know, you amaze me," Carrie marveled. "I mean, it would never even occur to me to walk away when I wanted to buy something just because I didn't like the salesperson. How do you acquire that kind of confidence?"

"You get raised by Katerina Cresswell," Emma replied.

Carrie shook her head. "Your mother and my mother are so totally different. My mother would have wanted Rage to have the sale because she's a struggling artist."

"Kat Cresswell doesn't know the meaning of struggle," Emma said with exaggerated hauteur.

"Oh, darling, I do *so* agree!" Carrie uttered, doing an exaggerated imitation of Emma's mother. "Struggle is just so . . . so petty!"

Emma laughed and looked at her watch. "Wow, I have to run. I'll call you!" She took off in the direction of the Hewitts's BMW.

Well, this is a reasonably good day, she thought. *I haven't seen Diana, and I haven't thought about Kurt for at least five minutes.*

FIVE

"Kurt, I have to tell you the truth," Emma whispered, staring into his eyes. "I still love you. I've tried not to, and I know you hate me—"

"No, I don't," Kurt interrupted her. He took her hand. "Don't you know I've been thinking about you every day? Every night?"

"Oh, Kurt—"

"I understand now, Em," he said earnestly. "You didn't do it because you don't love me; you did it because you're not ready to get married. I shouldn't have pushed you—"

Tears came to Emma's eyes. "I'm so sorry I hurt you. I'd rather die than hurt you—"

"Emma," he said huskily, and took her into his arms, kissing her until she was so dizzy she couldn't think or breathe. Then he lifted her in his muscular arms, and—

"Hey, Emma!" Sam called, shaking her. "Did you actually fall asleep?"

Emma opened her eyes, and slowly her dream about Kurt began to fade. "Go away," she instructed Sam, closing her eyes again blissfully. *Kurt is lifting me up in his muscular arms, my arms are around his neck, and—*

"From the grin on your face it must be a really dirty dream." Sam guffawed, pulling Emma's baseball cap down over her forehead.

"I don't want to be awake!" Emma protested, her eyes still closed. "I like my fantasies better than reality!"

"Let her dream, then," Carrie suggested good-naturedly.

"Well, okay," Sam said in a loud voice, "but you're going to miss hearing about me and Pres doing the wild thing on this very beach last night."

Emma opened her eyes and focused at last. "You're kidding."

"True," Sam admitted with a wicked grin, "but at least I got your attention."

Emma groaned and sat up. It was two nights later, and the three girls had arranged to meet at the beach at sunset. They had a radio, a cooler of drinks and some munchies, and they'd spread out an old beach blanket down near the water's edge. It was an unusually warm night, and they could faintly hear voices from the back of the Play Café.

"Pass me a diet Coke," Carrie asked Sam, since the cooler was closer to her.

Sam reached into the cooler and tossed a can to Carrie. "So, as I was saying, last night was unbelievably, incredibly, completely, marvelously, over-the-top romantic." She sighed blissfully at the memory of it.

"So?" Carrie prompted, opening her can of Coke. "As Sam Bridges would say, gimme the details!"

"You wanna hear details, too, O Boston baroness?" Sam asked Emma.

"Sure," Emma replied. "You live in the real world, I live in fantasy."

"It doesn't have to be that way, you know," Sam said, reaching into a bag of chips. "My brother, Adam, is crazed for you. He'd show up on the island in a New York minute, if you wiggled your pristine little finger in his direction."

"I just can't right now," Emma mumbled, digging her fingers into the sand.

"But I thought the two of you were about to become this major item," Sam said, reaching for some more chips.

"I thought maybe we were, too," Emma admitted. "But . . . something is stopping me."

"You mean someone," Carrie clarified.

"Okay, I mean someone," Emma agreed with a sigh.

"You've really got to just get over Kurt," Carrie said gently. "I mean, it really is over, you know."

"Oh, I know that," Emma said. "It's my heart that doesn't seem to know it." She sifted a handful of sand through her fingers. "Look, ignore me. I'm boring." She looked over at Sam. "Tell us about you and Pres."

"Hot night, isn't it?" Sam commented, taking a swig from a can of iced tea.

"You're stalling," Carrie said, poking Sam in the ribs.

"Just building the dramatic tension," Sam intoned mysteriously.

"Yo, Patrick, bring me out a brew, man!" someone yelled from the beach behind the Play Café.

"You're cut off, bud," another voice yelled. "You're supposed to be the designated driver!"

"Oh, drive this, jerk!" the first guy yelled back. "Get me a damn beer!"

"Gee, that's lovely," Carrie said sarcastically.

"No, that is a Neanderthal," Sam corrected Carrie. "Now Pres, he's lovely. Last night he came over on his motorcycle and took me to the Lobster Pound, where we ate mussels out of each other's fingers."

"Sounds slimy," Carrie commented.

"It was," Sam agreed with a laugh. "But sexy, too. And then he took me on his motorcycle to a reading at the Community Center," Sam continued.

"A *reading*?" Emma echoed.

"Yes, Miss Cresswell," Sam said, affecting the supercilious tones of a tweedy English professor, "a reading. Where an author reads from his work. I know you two lowlifes have never been to one."

Emma laughed. "Actually, I have, but—"

"So who was the author?" Carrie asked with curiosity.

"Who cares?" Sam asked. "You think I actually paid attention?"

Emma and Carrie both cracked up.

"And then," Sam continued dreamily, "he took me on his motorcycle to the wild and spectacular backyard of the Flirts' house."

"He didn't," Carrie challenged.

"He did," Sam replied, "where we romantically checked out the fireflies together, while consuming cool drinks and strawberries."

"Sounds terrif," Carrie commented.

"Yes, really lovely," Emma agreed politely.

Sam gave her a look. "You sound like you're thanking me for a tea party or something."

Emma shrugged. "No, it really does sound nice. I suppose I'm just jealous."

"Not jealous," Carrie pointed out. "Envious."

Emma nodded and hugged her knees to her chin.

Sam sighed. "I gotta tell you, Em, this Kurt stuff is making you really morose."

Emma sighed and stared out at the black ocean. *I know that what Sam's saying is true,* she realized. *It's like he's still got a hold of my heart. There's so much I still have to say to him, though I don't even dare write to him. But he's gone now, off in Michigan, and then to Colorado to the Air Force Academy. It'll never happen, and that's probably for the best. So why can't I stop thinking about him? Why can't I just get on with my life?*

Emma felt Sam's hand on her arm. "You're a hurting puppy, huh?" she said quietly.

Emma nodded. She felt tears threatening her eyes. "I'm sorry. I know I'm being an idiot—"

"We're just sorry that you feel so badly," Carrie said sympathetically. "Didn't it help when you went to see that therapist, Mrs. Miller?"

"I thought it did," Emma said. "But now I'm not so sure." She wiped angrily at the tears in the corners of her eyes. "Oh, I hate it when I get like this! Just ignore me!" She looked over at Sam. "I really, truly am happy that you and Pres are back together again."

Sam cocked her head to one side. "Are you?"

"Of course!" Emma exclaimed.

Sam pushed a strand of hair off her face. "I know this is nuts, but once I thought that maybe you and Pres were . . . you know."

"Pres and I are just friends," Emma said firmly.

"Yeah, well, I told you it was dumb," Sam said.

As Sam reached into the cooler for another can of iced tea, Emma turned away from her. *I'm never, ever going to tell Sam about that time Pres kissed me and, let's face it, I kissed him back,* she vowed. *It was*

one of the most terrible things I ever did,
risking my friendship with Sam like that.
It only happened because I was so confused
about Kurt. And it will never happen
again.

"You know, sometimes I can't believe
Pres and I are really back together," Sam
said softly, dropping her guard.

"I told you," Carrie said to her. "All you
had to do was stop flirting with everything
in pants and then let it happen."

"I'm letting it, I'm letting it," Sam said.
"And I'm liking it. A lot. Meanwhile, what
about you and Billy?"

"What about us?" Carrie asked.

"Well, now that you've both had negative
HIV tests and he doesn't have leukemia
after all, are you ready to, like, go for the
gusto?"

Carrie drank down some Coke. "I think
so. . . ."

"Yowza!" Sam chortled. "Go for it! Take
photos! Keep a journal! No, make a video!"

"You're so demented." Emma laughed.

"Hold up," Carrie said. "We're both feel-
ing a little weird because of Sly having
AIDS and everything," Carrie explained.
"It kind of spooked us."

Sam sighed and dug her toes into the
sand. "Can you imagine what it was like in

the sixties and seventies, when everyone was having sex with everyone and no one had to worry about dying from it?"

"I'm not so sure that was actually terrific, either," Carrie said. "My mom told me she thinks a lot of girls back then had sex with guys because they thought it was hip or politically correct or something, not because they were in love or anything."

"Who knows?" Emma asked. "I know nothing about guys or love or sex at all."

"Hey," Sam said, "let's lighten up! We are three hot babes on one hot night!"

But the mood didn't change much. All three girls just sat there, staring at the ocean, thinking about Sly, about guys, life and love. They didn't even notice when a young couple approached them stealthily, sneaking up on their hands and knees, their approach covered by the sound of the crashing waves.

And they didn't see the two water balloons being launched at them.

"Ahhhhhgh!" Sam screamed, jumping up, water dripping from her everywhere.

"Who did that?" Emma shrieked, water dripping off her baseball cap.

"I'm soaked!" Carrie cried, shaking herself so that water drops flew in all directions.

"Banzai!" a male voice yelled, and another balloon scored a direct hit on Sam's head.

The two attackers, rather than run away, ran at the girls. It was Jake Fisher and Erin Kane, laughing hysterically. "You should see the three of you!" Erin choked out between peals of laughter.

The three girls looked at each other's dripping hair, and when they realized how funny they looked, they all broke into smiles.

"Oh, well, it *is* a hot night," Carrie said good-naturedly.

"But we're definitely gonna get you guys back for this," Sam added, wagging her finger at Jake and Erin.

Are the two of them out together as friends, or are they on a date? Emma wondered, as she dripped all over the blanket.

"Someone in the café told us you were down here," Jake explained, "and we couldn't resist." He put his arm around Erin's shoulders, and she leaned against him.

My, my, Emma thought. *I guess it is a date. Which means that Jake Fisher has gone from dating Diana De Witt to dating Erin Kane. Wow.*

*   *   *

"Emma!" Ethan Hewitt called from the bottom of the stairs. "Telephone! For you!"

Emma had actually awakened a few minutes earlier and had been lying in bed, thinking about the evening before. She, Carrie, and Sam had ended up hanging out with Erin and Jake, and it was so hot that all of them had put on bathing suits and taken a midnight swim. After all, they were already soaking wet.

"Got it!" Emma yelled, as she heard Ethan barreling up the stairs to repeat the message. She reached over and picked up the phone.

I'll bet it's Sam, Emma thought, *calling to talk about last night. She probably can't believe Jake and Erin are dating, either!*

"Emma Cresswell," Emma said into the phone, immediately reverting to her oh-so-proper tones without giving it a thought.

"Emma darling!" an Australian-accented woman's voice called. "How wonderful to hear your voice again."

"Who is this?" Emma asked, not recognizing the voice.

"Why, it's Gillian Garrett, darling," the woman said. "Let's wake up, shall we?"

Gillian Garrett! Emma thought with surprise. *I never really expected to hear from her again. This is a pleasant surprise. Last time I spoke to Gillian I was in New York City, and I ended up modeling for an advertisement through her agency.*

Gillian, Emma recalled, ran one of the top modeling agencies in New York City and was a dear friend of Emma's Aunt Liz in New York. Earlier in the summer, when Emma was in the city, Gillian had booked Emma to appear in a photo shoot with Shannon Berman, the first woman to play major league baseball for the New York Mets, in an advertisement for a nail product. The photo and advertisement had actually appeared in one of the New York tabloid newspapers.

But I told Gillian I didn't want to model anymore, Emma recalled. *She said I was crazy, but I thought she understood I was serious. I wonder why she's calling me? Anyway, I like her. She's really, really nice.*

"Hello, Gillian," Emma said. "How are you? Where are you calling me from?"

"Just wonderful, love," Gillian answered, her voice full of her usual enthusiasm. "And I'm in New York, where else? It's the center of the universe."

Emma laughed. "That's a matter of opinion," she said. "I prefer Paris."

"You've got a point," Gillian agreed. "Listen, I'll cut right to the chase. I'm calling about a job."

"A job?" Emma said doubtfully. "Thank you for thinking of me," she said politely. "But my job is here, and I'm really not comfortable with the idea of getting paid for how I look."

"Just so," Gillian answered.

"So is it a modeling job?" Emma asked.

"Yes," Gillian answered, a note of levity in her voice, "it is."

"Then I'm not interested, because—"

"It's at a good location," Gillian offered.

"Where?" Emma asked, purely out of courtesy.

"Oh, an island off the coast of Maine called Sunset Island, or some such thing," Gillian answered breezily.

Emma felt her interest pique.

No, Emma said to herself. *I made myself a promise.*

"Not interested," Emma replied.

"It's for a good cause," Gillian wheedled.

Emma couldn't help herself. "What do you mean?"

"You've heard of *Beautiful* magazine?" Gillian asked.

"Of course," Emma replied. "I read somewhere recently that it's outselling *Cosmopolitan* now. And I like their ideas that promote beauty as being all different sizes and ages and races and shapes," Emma continued, "but it's still not my idea of a good cause."

"Did you know that Miranda Swertzel, the editor-in-chief of *Beautiful* has rheumatoid arthritis?" Gillian continued, ignoring Emma's remark.

"I think I read that somewhere, too," Emma said. "What are you getting at?" She switched the phone to the other ear.

"*Beautiful* is planning a full-court press against the disease," Gillian explained. "Did you know that it strikes mostly women between the ages of twenty and forty?"

"No, I didn't," Emma admitted. "I don't really know very much about it."

"Exactly the problem, darling," Gillian continued dramatically. "Because it cripples rather than kills, and because it affects women so much more often than men, it doesn't get a great deal of attention. Well, *Beautiful* is creating a campaign showing various types of beautiful women and reminding the world that a percentage of them have this disease, and a larger percentage will get it before the age of forty. It's really very important."

"And they're shooting on Sunset Island?"

"That's what they specified to me," Gillian answered. "Miranda has a house there. They plan to shoot it on the beach, so all the girls and women in the ad will look healthy and be frolicking in the sun and all that. The point is that it's a disease people can't see."

"Really," Emma murmured.

"Listen, darling, I've decided to waive my entire compensation for this one, because it's truly a cause I believe in," Gillian continued. "My sister has R.A. It ruined her dancing career. And I've seen her suffer and be in and out of a wheelchair, and she's only twenty-five."

"That's terrible!" Emma commiserated.

"I want you involved," Gillian said. "So does Liz," she added.

"Why is that?" Emma asked.

"Because she has it," Gillian said simply.

Emma's heart beat faster. "What do you mean, Aunt Liz has it?" Emma asked.

"She was diagnosed with it last year," Gillian reported.

"Well, she never told me!" Emma exclaimed.

"Exactly," Gillian said. "She didn't want you to know. But I have a big mouth, and she'll probably kill me for telling you. Now, can you do it?"

"Is Liz okay?" Emma asked with trepidation.

"So far," Gillian said. "She has some bad days when she's exhausted. And she's stiff in the morning. But right now she's fairly well controlled with a lot of awful medication with truly dreary side effects."

"I have to call her—" Emma began.

"Darling, please," Gillian interrupted. "I wasn't supposed to tell you. Wait until she tells you herself. I just wanted to impress upon you why I would like you involved in this."

Emma thought a moment. *This isn't really like modeling for advertisements. And I wouldn't actually have to take any money. Oh, God, I can't believe Aunt Liz is sick and she never even told me!*

"All right," Emma finally agreed. "I'll do it. But I won't take any money."

"Splendid," Gillian said. "We're shooting in three days. I'd like you to assemble some girls my photographer and I can take a look at. I'm calling an agency in Portland, but if you've anyone you think I should see, I'd be delighted."

"Any specific type?" Emma asked.

"It doesn't matter," Gillian replied, "as long as they're beautiful. That's the whole point of the campaign."

"I'll ask a few friends," Emma promised.

"We'll supply all the clothing, accessories, all that sort of thing," Gillian promised. "I'm arriving at the Sunset Inn that morning. Call me there."

"Okay," Emma agreed.

"I'm excited about this one," Gillian said. "It's such a wonderful cause. Even the photographer is doing it for free."

"That's great," Emma answered, looking at her clock. She had exactly ten minutes to get up, get washed and dressed, and get downstairs to help the kids with their breakfast.

"He's wonderful, darling," Gillian continued in her gushing fashion. "A real comer, and getting quite famous. I haven't even met him myself yet, but I've certainly seen his work. Perhaps you've heard of him."

"David Frohman?" Emma asked hopefully, naming a Pulitzer prize–winning photographer who she, Sam and Carrie had actually met.

"I wish!" Gillian exclaimed gaily. "But almost as good. Darling, I can't believe our luck. We've managed to snare the one and only Flash Hathaway. Bye now!"

Emma heard the *click*, and she just sat there, staring at the phone.

She knew Flash Hathaway. He was the

sleaziest cretin who'd ever oozed behind a camera.

No good deed shall go unpunished, Emma thought to herself, remembering something she'd heard her mother say long ago. *I can't believe what I just did. I agreed, voluntarily, to work with Flash Hathaway.*

SIX

"Say cheese, babe!"

"I don't want to say cheese," Emma said through clenched teeth.

"When the Flash Man says say cheese, you don't say no, babe."

Emma and Carrie cracked up at Sam's perfect imitation of Flash Hathaway, the lecherous photographer who was going to do the shoot for Gillian Garrett and the National Arthritis Foundation. The three girls were all hanging out by the pool in Graham Perry Templeton's lavish backyard. At the moment, they were all sitting at the edge of the pool, dangling their feet into the water.

It was late afternoon, and Emma had just told her friends about the upcoming photo shoot. She didn't mention what Gillian had told her about Aunt Liz having rheumatoid arthritis—she didn't think she should until Liz told her, herself. Sam was chaperoning Becky Jacobs, who had begged Sam to drive her to the Templeton's after camp, so she could hang out with Ian. Emma was actually free for the day, as Jane and Jeff Hewitt had made a quick trip home with their kids.

"Say cheese for the Flash Man, babe!" Sam repeated, mimicking Flash's New York accent perfectly. "And while you're at it, show me your hooters!"

Emma rolled her eyes. "I know it's for a good cause, but I can't believe I said I'd do this job," she lamented.

"How is it that the slime lizard keeps getting work?" Sam wondered.

"Because while he may be a scummy human being, he's a really good photographer," Carrie explained.

"So?" Sam countered. "You're a better photographer and you're a terrific human being. I say you should get all his work."

Carrie smiled. "I wish."

Emma kicked her feet in the water. "Honestly, if I'd known Flash was going to be the photographer, I'd never have agreed to do this shoot. What am I getting myself into?"

"He loves you," Sam snorted. "He wants you to bear his children."

Emma splashed her playfully. "Oh, thank you *so* much."

"Actually, he loves *you*," Carrie countered, looking at Sam.

Sam winced. "Don't remind me."

Emma stared at Sam. *I guess she's thinking about the time he talked her into posing in sleazy, see-through lingerie,* Emma recalled. *The photos were supposed to be for Sam's modeling portfolio. But then Flash blew up the shots without her permission and displayed them at a raunchy strip club. Poor Sam was so humiliated!*

Then, Flash appeared as the official photographer for Flirting With Danger's big East Coast tour, Emma remembered. *That time Flash took photos of Sam with rock star Johnny Angel that made it look as if they were sleeping together, which they weren't. Those pictures almost wrecked Sam's relationship with Pres forever.*

"Maybe he's reformed?" Carrie suggested, though she sounded very dubious.

"Ha, right," Sam snorted. "And maybe Diana De Witt's gonna join a convent. Hey, I've got a great idea!"

"What?" Emma asked.

"Send the two of them to the shoot," Sam said, cocking her head toward Becky and

Ian, who were sunning themselves on lounges as far away from their au pairs as possible, listening to tapes of their band, Lord Whitehead and the Zit People, on twin headphones. "Make sure that Ian's entire band is invited to provide the music. Even Flash couldn't take that," Sam said.

"Now that Becky is busy being a C.I.T., Ian is really missing her," Carrie said.

Emma watched Ian lean over and kiss Becky. "Young love," she said, sighing.

"Oh yeah, like you're over the hill." Sam laughed. "On second thought, we'd better not send Becky to see Flash. He's so sleazy he'd probably hit on her."

"Is there any way you can get out of this, Emma?" Carrie asked.

"Not really," Emma replied. "I already gave Gillian my word. Anyway, you two will be there, right?"

"No can do, babe," Sam barked, imitating another one of Flash's patented sayings. "I've got to hang with the monsters the day of the shoot because there's no camp that day."

"Great," Emma replied, "abandon me in my hour of need." She looked at Carrie hopefully.

"Sorry," Carrie said with a shrug. "I'm

stuck with Chloe all that day. Graham and Claudia are going to Portland with Ian."

Emma threw her hand over her eyes. "I'm going to be there all alone!"

"Gee, I'm missing out on hours with Flash," Sam commented. "I'm crushed."

"Maybe Darcy will come," Carrie suggested, referring to Darcy Laken, one of the girls' best friends on the island. "And Molly."

Sam gave Carrie a look. "Molly is in a wheelchair."

"So?" Carrie asked. "Didn't Emma tell us that Gillian asked for all different types of beauty?"

"I don't think she meant the physically challenged," Sam pointed out dryly. She glanced over at Ian and Becky, who were now mid-kiss. "Do I need to break that up?"

"Trust me," Carrie said. "If they're doing it in front of us, it's harmless."

"I will invite Darcy and Molly," Emma decided, "and I'll ask Erin when we see her tonight."

Erin had invited the three girls over to her uncle's house for a cookout. It would be a chance for them to meet her folks, she'd said.

"Oh, come on," Sam exclaimed. "I really

87

like the girl, but you can't invite Erin to an audition for a modeling job! She's fat!"

"I told you, Gillian said she wanted all types," Emma repeated patiently.

"Yeah, right," Sam replied sarcastically. "Gillian's just being p.c."

"I don't think she's just being politically correct," Carrie said. "Besides, there are full-figured models, you know."

"Who'd want to be a full-figured model?" Sam asked. "I mean, why wouldn't you just want to lose the weight?"

Carrie blanched. "It's not so easy, Sam."

"I didn't mean you!" Sam said quickly. "You're not fat!"

"Well, I'm certainly not thin," Carrie said. "And next to models, I feel like a cow."

"You're curvy!" Sam protested. "Anyway, there's a difference between being extra curvy and being forty pounds overweight."

"I wish you'd quit harping on Erin's weight," Emma said sharply.

Sam gave her a look. "Since when are you a defender of the oversized?"

"Well, you don't sound that different from Diana, if you really want to know," Emma continued, anger in her voice. "The only difference is that Diana says nasty things to Erin's face, and you say them behind her back."

Sam looked hurt. "Is that really what you think?"

"Look, all I'm saying is that you could be kinder," Emma said in a softer tone. "And more open-minded."

"Erin certainly doesn't have any trouble attracting guys," Carrie pointed out.

"And Jake is a major fox," Sam mused. "I can't figure out why he likes her."

"See, there you go again!" Emma exclaimed. "He likes her because she's nice and smart and talented and pretty, would be my guess. He likes her for the same reasons Pres likes you."

"Well, all I can say is, I'm glad I'm not overweight," Sam said a little petulantly.

"If you were," Carrie said, "we'd still love you."

"Maybe so," Sam commented, looking over at Ian and Becky, who were kissing again. "But I'm not sure I'd love me."

Maybe that, Emma thought to herself, *is one of your basic problems.* But she kept her mouth shut.

"So, Erin told us you're a nose," Sam said to Mr. Kane, as she sat down on one of the rocking chairs that graced the back porch at Erin's aunt and uncle's house.

Marshall Kane, Erin's dad, laughed heartily. "That's right," he replied. "Sounds like I'd just be a huge walking schnozz, doesn't it?"

All the girls cracked up.

Erin has such a normal family, Emma thought, as she sat in one of the other rockers. *Sort of like Carrie's family, except that Erin is an only child. I just can't believe that Erin's father doesn't have a job anymore!*

The girls had all met, as planned, at Erin's aunt and uncle's house at seven. It was a weathered Cape–Cod styled house on the eastern end of the island. Unassuming, and even a little ramshackle from the front, the house had a spectacular rear area—the back porch looked out on a lawn which ended in cliffs that dropped precipitously down to the bay below.

Emma, Sam, and Carrie were hanging out on the back porch with Erin and her folks. Erin's aunt and uncle were in Portland for the evening. Jake was stopping by after dinner, Erin had told them. In the meantime, Erin's mother, Karen Kane, was minding the barbecue at the end of the porch, where pieces of chicken and shrimps covered with homemade barbecue sauce were sizzling away.

"Is it fun making perfume?" Carrie asked Mr. Kane.

Erin's dad got a faraway look in his eyes. "It is the most wonderful thing in the world," he said. "And you know what the best part is?"

"Giving free samples to his daughter," Erin cracked.

"That's the second best part," Marshall Kane said with a smile, running his fingers over his bald scalp. As Erin had intimated to the girls, Mr. Kane was totally bald—it looked to Emma like he actually shaved his head. But he was as striking looking as his daughter, with piercing blue eyes and a muscular build for a man of nearly fifty years old. Emma looked over at Erin's mom, a very pretty, plump woman in her mid-forties.

I guess maybe Erin inherited her weight from her mom, Emma thought.

"The best part," Mr. Kane continued, "is when I'm walking down the street of some city, and four or five women in a row pass by me wearing a perfume that I invented."

"Has that happened to you?" Carrie asked.

"Not really," Mr. Kane admitted. "The most I ever counted on one street was three."

They all rocked companionably and watched gulls making lazy circles in the sky for a few minutes.

"You know what would be great?" Sam said dreamily, staring out over the water. "A perfume that smelled like the ocean."

"Ah, dead fish!" Erin cried.

"No, you know what I mean," Sam said. "Like the magic of the ocean, something like that."

"Very poetic," Mr. Kane said with a grin. "The magic of the ocean. I like that."

Somewhere inside the house a phone rang. "I'll get it," Erin's mom called, and she hurried into the house.

"I don't really wear perfume," Carrie admitted. She looked over at Mr. Kane. "I hope that doesn't offend you."

"I consider girls like you a challenge," Mr. Kane said, "because I believe there is a scent for everyone. I mean, we have five senses. Think of all the joy your sense of smell gives to you! Think what a perfume can do for you!"

"What?" Carrie asked blankly.

Mr. Kane pretended to hold his heart. "You don't feel the love song of fragrance, huh?"

"Frankly, no," Carrie admitted. "Sorry."

"Oh, ignore her," Sam said. "She's too practical for her own good. Now me, I love perfume, but most of it's way expensive."

"It doesn't have to be expensive to be good," Mr. Kane said. "Sometimes the pricey ones have a major ad campaign, and that's what you're paying for."

"Not rare flowers or something like that?" Sam asked.

"Not always," Mr. Kane explained.

"I did wear StarStruck," Sam told Mr. Kane. "I liked it."

"But you didn't love it," Mr. Kane said.

"This guy I was dating did," Sam said with a shrug. "But . . . I don't know. I'm different now then I was when I wore that."

"That's why I was looking for a new perfume myself the other day," Emma said quietly. "Because I'm different now than I was when I started wearing the perfume my mother had made for us."

"So, what kind of scent are you looking for?" Mr. Kane asked eagerly.

Something that will bring Kurt back to me, popped into Emma's mind.

"Well, I'm not really sure," she said.

"Something romantic? Sensual, maybe? Or innocent?" Mr. Kane prompted Emma eagerly.

"Uh, Dad? Maybe we should talk about something else," Erin suggested.

She's worried that he's going to get upset talking about perfume after he just got fired from his job, Emma realized.

Mr. Kane smiled fondly at his daughter. "Oh, you know me. I'm addicted to even talking about perfume. If I can't make it anymore, at least I can talk about it."

"You'll get another job!" Erin insisted.

Mr. Kane patted his daughter's hand.

"Well," Sam said, jokingly, "if you ever want to make one, Emma here can finance the whole project, and Carrie and me can figure out how to sell it."

"Carrie and I," Carrie corrected before she could stop herself.

"Whatever," Sam said breezily. "No one will fix my grammar after I've made my first million." She reached for her glass of lemonade. "I can just see it now—that incredibly sexy new fragrance, 'Sam!' And I do all the modeling for the TV commercials, and I become mega-famous and incredibly rich, and Christian Slater and Johnny Angel are both begging me to marry them—"

"Don't mind her," Carrie said. "She has a rich fantasy life."

"We'd get all the best tables at the best restaurants," Sam continued, on a roll. "My picture would be on the cover of *Sassy* and *Seventeen* and, hey, why not *Vogue* and *Mademoiselle* and *Glamour* . . . "

". . . as well as the *New York Times Magazine* and *Businessweek*," Erin joked.

". . . and every girl in America would envy me, and I'd never have to work as an au pair again," Sam concluded. She looked around at her friends. "This is really a good plan."

"Uh, I believe it's called a dream, not a plan," Erin pointed out.

"Well, so what?" Sam asked. "Every plan starts with a dream—right, Mr. Kane?"

"Right," he agreed. "I like the way you think!"

"Well, you know," Carrie said in her usual reasonable tone of voice. "It's not all that impossible."

Everyone turned to look at her.

"I mean, theoretically," Carrie continued, reaching down for her own glass of lemonade. "Mr. Kane could create it, you and I could do the design work and, well, Emma could . . ."

"Finance it," Emma said, grinning. "Just out of curiosity, what would it cost?"

"A lot," Mr. Kane replied. "How much do you have?"

"A lot-a lot," Sam answered for her.

Mr. Kane got that faraway look in his eyes again. "Well, it's a nice dream. I could work something out with John Goldman in New Jersey. . . ."

"Who's he?" Sam demanded.

"Oh, a fellow I know with a laboratory," Mr. Kane replied. "A good friend, actually." He still had that look in his eyes. "Imagine. Creating the world's most wonderful perfume with my own company. Working for myself. Keeping the product pure and natural. Keeping the price low because there wouldn't be all that corporate overhead. . . ." He blinked quickly and focused on the girls again. "Well, anyway, it's a really nice dream."

Erin stood up and raised her glass of lemonade.

"A toast," she said. "Raise your glasses."

"What to?" Sam asked.

"To dreams," she said, giving her dad a

loving look. "It's what keeps us all going sometimes."

They all raised their glasses together.

"To dreams!"

SEVEN

"That dinner was fabulous," Carrie told Erin's mom. "I am stuffed."

"I'm glad you liked it," Karen Kane said with a smile. "The secret is the barbecue sauce."

"She won't even tell me what's in it," Erin said, pretending to pout. "And here I thought mothers were supposed to hand their recipes down to their daughters."

"Well, you hate to cook," Mrs. Kane said with a laugh. "I'll tell you what, if you ever get married I'll pass it down to your husband."

"Sorry I missed the feast," Jake said. He was sitting next to Erin on the back porch swing, his arm around her shoulders. He had arrived just as the group was having coffee, tea, and homemade pecan pie.

"Next time I'll invite you for the whole shebang," Erin promised him.

He kissed her forehead. "I'll hold you to it," he said.

"So, what do you think about our scheme to get rich and famous?" Sam asked Jake, polishing off her huge slice of pie.

They had just finished telling Jake about the conversation they'd had about creating a perfume.

"What, are you really serious about it?" Jake asked.

"Of course not," Mr. Kane said quickly. "How could I possibly expect my daughter's friend to finance something like that?"

"Venture capitalists do it all the time," Emma said mildly, sipping her tea.

"Maybe," Mr. Kane agreed, "but you aren't a venture capitalist."

"Well, maybe I could be," Emma replied.

Mr. Kane stood up. "It's kind of you to say so," he told Emma. "Like I said, we all live on dreams." He turned to his wife. "Come on, let's you and me go in and watch that video I rented and leave the kids alone."

"I'd love to," Mrs. Kane said, standing up and reaching for her husband's hand.

"Listen, I know I'm a pig, but can I snitch another piece of pie?" Sam asked. "It's delish!"

"Help yourself," Mrs. Kane said, and

then she and her husband went into the house.

"Anyone else want another piece?" Sam asked, as she walked over to the table and cut herself a second generous slice.

"It must be fun to have your metabolism," Erin said easily. "I'd love to be able to eat whatever I want and never gain any weight."

"It's probably because I'm so active that I can eat like a horse," Sam explained, bringing her pie back to the rocking chair. "Maybe you need to exercise more."

Emma kicked Sam so that Erin couldn't see.

"Well, you don't have to do anything," Sam added quickly, realizing her blunder. "I mean, you should do what you want to, is what I mean. I think." She stuffed her mouth with a huge bite of pie.

"Let's talk about perfume," Emma said, smoothly changing the subject. "I wonder what it really would cost to start up a perfume."

"Are you serious?" Erin asked her.

Emma nodded.

"If you're serious, really serious," Erin said slowly, "I'm sure my dad could find out for you."

"Okay," Emma agreed.

Erin gave Emma a funny look. "I hope this isn't an awkward question or anything, but just how rich are you?"

"She's only one of the richest heiresses in the country," Sam said, taking another forkful of pie.

"Sam, Emma can answer for herself," Carrie said in a low voice.

"Well, I'm just saving her the trouble," Sam explained breezily. "Besides, I like saying it. 'One of the richest heiresses in the country,'" Sam repeated reverently. "I only wish it were me."

Erin pushed some of her curls off her face. "But why would you be interested in going into the perfume business, if you don't mind my asking."

Emma shrugged. "I don't know. Maybe I'm not. But the idea of all of us creating something together really appeals to me. I've always thought it was a total waste to just have money sitting around doing nothing."

"Donate it to charity," Jake suggested.

"I do," Emma said. "But this is something else." She took another sip of her tea. "Besides, I hate what happened to your dad, Erin. It's totally unfair. And maybe I can help do something about it."

"I'm gonna be famous!" Sam cheered.

"Down, girl," Carrie said with a laugh. "We aren't calling the perfume 'Sam.'"

"We aren't?" Sam asked wistfully.

"No," Carrie stated. "We're calling it 'Zit,' the only designer fragrance endorsed by the infamous band Lord Whitehead and the Zit People."

"What would be a really good name?" Emma mused.

Carrie gave Emma a look. "Wait a second. *Are* you really serious about this? Or are you just fooling around?"

"You all keep asking me that, but the truth is, I haven't had a chance to give it real thought," Emma admitted. "I'd need more facts and figures. But it's fun to think about, right?"

And it keeps my mind off Kurt, she added to herself.

"Okay, okay, I've got it!" Sam exclaimed. "The perfect name for a perfume!"

"What's that?" Erin asked.

"DIANA!" Sam uttered reverentially. "And the ad copy will read, 'You, too, can smell like a slut!'" Just at that moment, Sam remembered that Jake had dated Diana. "Oops . . ." she said, turning red.

"Hey, I only went out with her once," Jake said, holding his palms up, "and she asked me. After that I never returned the invitation."

Erin grinned at him. "That shows great taste on your part."

He smiled back at her. "I agree."

They really like each other, Emma thought. *I remember how that feels, when a relationship is new and everything seems possible. Now all I feel is sad and kind of dead.* She gulped hard. *Maybe I really should do something with this perfume. Maybe I need something that would be so engrossing, I wouldn't have time to feel sad. . . .*

"It's getting chilly, huh?" Carrie said, reaching for the denim jacket slung over the back of her rocking chair.

Emma nodded and slipped the sweater she'd brought with her over her head. The endless hot weather was finally breaking as a cold front moved in from the west. She could see the clouds building from west to east as the front cleared the Maine coastline and headed east into the Atlantic, over Sunset Island.

Even the bad weather makes me think of Kurt, Emma realized. *Like the time we had a picnic in his backyard during a storm, or the time—*

"Smells kinda like rain," Jake commented, sniffing the air and snuggling closer to Erin.

"Kinda Like Rain," Erin mused. "Good name for a Native American character in a Western movie. Crappy name for a perfume."

Everyone laughed.

"Oh, you think it's so funny!" Erin exclaimed. "When your father is a nose, you don't discuss current events at the dinner table, you think up perfume names! How about 'Gums' for that beautiful toothless woman. Or 'Passing Wind' for the flatulent set."

"Stop! You're killing me!" Sam cried, bent over with laughter.

Jake hugged Erin and then he kissed her lightly. "You are fabulous," he said in a low voice, but Emma had overheard.

He doesn't seem to have any problem with her weight at all, Emma thought. *And he's a guy that most girls would call extremely cute!* Emma looked over at Sam and saw that Sam was checking out Erin and Jake together as well. *Can you blame him for liking her? I think Erin is as funny as Sam. . . .*

"I was thinking," Carrie said. "If we do actually do this thing, what if we marketed this nameless perfume right here on the island?"

"Starting small is probably a good idea," Jake said, nodding.

"But I don't like to start small," Sam complained. "I want to rule the world!"

"It's smart to start small," Erin said. "You guys could always get bigger later on."

Carrie looked at Erin. "What do you mean, 'you guys'? Aren't you in on this?"

"Nope," Erin said. "I am strictly a non-business type. Besides, I always vowed I wouldn't go into my father's business."

A flash of lightning lit up the sky.

"Hey, how about calling the perfume 'Lightning'?" Sam suggested.

"Nahhhh," Carrie replied, wrinkling her nose. "Too electric and jangly."

Another bolt of lightning streaked across the sky, followed by a clap of thunder.

"I love thunderstorms," Sam said dreamily, hugging herself.

"Me, too," Erin said. "They're romantic."

"Especially when they come with tornadoes," Sam added. "It's a spectator sport back where I'm from. They sell lottery tickets at shopping malls in Kansas to bet if the roofs stay on."

They were all quiet for a moment, watching the approaching storm.

"You know, selling the perfume on the island would really be a good idea," Emma finally said. "It would give us a chance to check out the product. That way we can make marketing and packaging adjustments, that sort of thing."

Everyone looked at her.

"Since when do you know so much about business?" Sam asked.

Emma shrugged. "I guess I've picked up more from my dad over the years than I realized. He wasn't born with any money, you know. He made it all himself."

"It's her mom who comes complete with the millions," Sam said mildly.

"That's right," Emma agreed. "Maybe I'm more like my father than I realized." She thought about that for a minute. "I have to say, the idea of starting my own business and making it work has a certain appeal to me."

Sam shook her head. "I don't get it. I don't see why anyone would work if they didn't have to."

A few drops of rain began to fall, and everyone moved back underneath the covered part of the porch. Jake and Erin didn't have to move, since they were already sitting under the awning. Jake leaned over and sniffed Erin's neck. "You smell so great. What perfume are you wearing?"

"Oh, nothing," Erin fibbed. "I wake up smelling like this."

He tickled her ribs.

"Okay, I lied," Erin said with a laugh. "Actually, it's a combination of essential oils and stuff that my dad had. I kind of mixed them together. It never comes out the same twice."

"Well, it's great," Jake said, sniffing her again.

"You know what I really hate?" Erin asked, nuzzling against Jake. "I hate it that all these fragrances you see are packaged with all this stuff on them, you know? I mean, you just rip all that stuff off and throw it away. It's so totally uncool for the environment!"

"Emma and I were just talking about that the other day!" Carrie exclaimed. "We were at the Cheap Boutique and all that stuff was totally overpackaged. It's such a waste!"

"And the companies charge more for all the waste, too!" Erin added passionately. "It makes me sick! Plus, some of these perfume and cosmetic companies test their ingredients out on animals. Now, how gross is that?"

"Did the company your father worked for do that?"

"No, I'm happy to say," Erin reported. "My father won't work for a company that does animal testing—which makes his employment possibilities even slimmer."

The rain slowed as the storm began to pass them by.

"Well, maybe soon your father won't need to be looking for a job at all," Emma said. "Maybe we really are going to do this."

"Cool," Jake commented.

Just at that moment, there was a screech of tires in the driveway in front of the house.

"What was that?" Sam asked.

"Beats me," Erin replied.

There was the sound of five or six loud bangs exploding from the same location. Everyone jumped to their feet.

"Was that a gun?" Emma asked fearfully.

"I think it was fireworks," Jake said.

All five of them ran to the front of the house. They could see Mr. and Mrs. Kane still inside, sitting in the living room watching their video.

They must not have heard, Emma thought to herself.

But there was nothing for the five of them to see on the front driveway. Whoever had lit the firecrackers had taken off quickly.

"What a stupid prank," Carrie said irritably, her hands on her hips. "How juvenile, to light off some fireworks and then drive off."

"Hey!" Sam yelled. "What's that?" She pointed to a carefully gift-wrapped package, about the size of two shoeboxes put together, lying at the side of the driveway. It was illuminated by the light coming from inside the house.

They ran over to it.

"There's a card on it," Sam said. She reached down and picked it up.

"'To Erin,'" she read.

"Careful, it might be a bomb," Jake warned.

"Oh, come on!" Erin laughed. "You've seen too many movies!" She quickly tore the wrapper open and looked inside.

There was a plastic container of a well-known diet shake mix. There were several Weight Watchers frozen entrees. There was an article torn from a popular magazine entitled, "Lose Weight and Make a

New You!" And taped to the top of the article was a note that read: "Hey, fatso, get a clue!"

"Diana De Witt," Sam muttered, her teeth clenched. "It has to be her. Man, I'd like to kill her." She turned to Erin. "I'm sorry."

"Why?" Erin asked, her voice shaky. "You didn't do anything."

"She's a bitch," Jake said in a low voice.

"It's no problem," Erin insisted, trying to force a smile to her lips. "Or rather it is a problem, but it's hers, not mine."

Emma smiled at Erin, and Erin smiled back. But Emma saw that Erin's lower lip was quavering uncontrollably.

"I'm sorry again about what happened tonight," Emma said quietly, as she and Erin walked together along the rain-dampened boardwalk just off of Sunset Island's main beach.

"Me, too," Erin replied, stopping for a moment to pick up a stray beer can that had worked its way into the middle of the boardwalk and dropping it into a nearby trashcan.

"They should have recycling bins out here," Erin commented.

Sam, Carrie, and Jake had all gone

home not long after the firecracker/diet package incident—Jake would have stayed, but he had agreed to help out some friends with a recording session over in Portland, and he had to catch the last ferry there.

Emma was about to go home, too, but at the last minute, decided to stay and see whether Erin wanted to go for a walk on the boardwalk with her. When she asked, Erin gratefully agreed. Just after they started walking, Emma had asked Erin about whether she wanted to come to the audition for the arthritis foundation benefit, and Erin had enthusiastically agreed. Now, the conversation had turned back to the ugly events of earlier in the evening.

"We don't have to talk about Diana if you don't want to," Emma said quietly.

Erin sighed. "I don't mind, really. It was kind of embarrassing. Okay, it was *really* embarrassing, especially in front of Jake."

"Well, if it's any consolation, he thinks less of her, not you," Emma pointed out.

Erin didn't reply, and the two walked along slowly in companionable silence.

"I really appreciate your asking me out here with you," Erin finally said. "It can be tough, you know? Being in a new place."

Emma nodded. "This is a good place to

think—something I've been doing a lot of lately. I've been going through a pretty rough time."

"You?" Erin asked with surprise. "It always seems like everything with you is just perfect."

"It isn't," Emma admitted. "It might seem like it, but it isn't."

"No?" Erin repeated. "How so?"

Emma hesitated. *I don't even know Erin very well. How much do I want to open up to her about what happened to me? On the other hand, I think I want her to be my friend. Oh, why not. The whole island knows anyway. If Erin doesn't hear it from me, she'll hear the story from someone else,* Emma thought.

"You're not the only person who broke up with their boyfriend this summer," Emma said diplomatically.

"Really?" Erin said. "Welcome to the club. What happened?"

Emma gave Erin the short version of the story with Kurt, leaving out the part about what happened at their wedding.

All in due time, Emma thought to herself. *I'm still not comfortable talking about that day. I don't know if I ever will be, either.*

"So," Emma concluded, "he's in Michigan with his cousin right now."

"Sounds pretty traumatic," Erin commented.

"I did get a letter from his father not long ago," Emma confided.

"What did it say?" Erin asked.

"He basically accused me of abusing his son," Emma replied.

"Ouch," Erin said sympathetically.

"Anyway," Emma said, "I'm sure I'll never see Kurt again. He's going to the Air Force Academy in Colorado Springs in the fall."

"Maybe it's better that way," Erin ventured.

Emma didn't reply, because it felt as if a knife was twisting into her heart. *I have to see Kurt again, I just have to,* she thought wildly. *Otherwise how can I go on with my life?*

"Are you seeing anyone else yet?" Erin asked her.

"I was," Emma admitted, picking up a stray seashell. "Sam's half-brother, Adam, actually."

"So, what happened?"

"I really liked him," Emma admitted. "But . . . well, I guess it's just too soon for me." She looked over at Erin. "Anyway, it seems like you've found a replacement pretty quickly for yours."

"Jake's great," Erin agreed. "I like him a lot, and I think he likes me. But who knows what will happen?"

"Well, he *definitely* likes you—anyone can see that," Emma commented, stopping to lean her hands on the rail of the boardwalk that overlooked the main beach and breathe in the rain-scrubbed, ocean-scented air.

Erin leaned against the railing, too, and stared out at the darkened sea. "What is it with Diana, Emma?" she asked in a soft voice. "I mean, she clearly hates my guts. What did I ever do to her? She doesn't even know me!"

"You're singing in the band instead of her," Emma reminded Erin, "and you're dating Jake and she's not."

"Well, she needs to just get a life . . . and get out of mine!" Erin exclaimed.

Emma shook her head. "Unfortunately, Diana likes to go for the jugular. You probably haven't heard the last of her."

"Meaning that she will live to humiliate me again," Erin translated with a groan.

"Probably," Emma replied honestly. She pushed some hair behind her ear. "If it's any consolation to you, she humiliates me,

Sam, and Carrie every chance she gets, too."

Erin tried to smile. "At least I'm in good company."

The two girls wandered over to a nearby bench and sat down. Emma threw the seashell she'd picked up toward the ocean.

"Have you ever been made fun of because of how you looked?" Erin asked softly, then she laughed. "No, I guess you never have, considering how you look."

"It must feel terrible," Emma said in a low voice.

"It sucks," Erin said fiercely. "Even if you're okay with how you look, it still totally sucks."

"I imagine so," Emma agreed.

"It's happened to me ever since I was a kid."

"Kids can be really cruel," Emma commiserated.

"It's not like I haven't tried to lose weight," Erin said passionately. "It's not like every single magazine and TV show and movie and everything else in the world doesn't scream at you and judge you if you're overweight! So I tried, tons of times. And I succeeded, too! I'd lose weight by starving myself, and then as soon as I started eating, I'd gain it back. Lose it, and gain it back. Only it seemed like each time I was a little fatter than the time before. It was the worst."

Emma didn't say anything.

"So finally," Erin continued, "I decided I had to try to be happy with myself the way I am." She was quiet for a moment. "And if you think that's so easy, think again."

"Because so many people are quick to tell you that you shouldn't be happy with yourself the way you are?" Emma asked.

Erin nodded. "And you know, girls are worse than guys about it, and that's the truth. Back in high school it was tough with guys, too. You know, it's not cool to date a 'fat chick,'" she added bitterly.

Emma winced. "That must have made you feel awful."

Erin shrugged. "It's much better in college. Guys are more grown up, more individual. I suppose there are guys who don't find me attractive because they think I'm too heavy, but there always seems to be cute guys interested in me, too."

"Well, for one thing, you're really pretty," Emma pointed out.

"Pretty and overweight," Erin replied, trying to smile. "I'm the type people always say 'she has such a pretty face' about. Anyway, I think I'm making progress."

"On losing weight?" Emma asked her.

"On being happy with myself the way I am," Erin said firmly, as she stared out at the ocean.

I wish I could say the same thing, Emma said to herself. *But the way I feel about Kurt, it's like there's a big hole in my heart, and I sometimes feel like I'll never be happy until that hole is fixed. Why can't I just accept what happened and move on? Why can't I?*

She looked back over at Erin, and she found herself envying the other girl.

EIGHT

". . . so," Emma concluded, glancing over at Erin, "that's the ugly story about Flash Hathaway and us. The end."

"Not the end," Erin pointed out, as Emma pulled the Hewitts's car into a parking space in the lot at the Sunset Inn. "After all, you're about to go in there and work with him again."

Emma turned off the car and turned to Erin. "I can't believe I have to look at his lecherous little face."

"Want to bail out now?" Erin asked.

"No." Emma sighed. "This is for a charity I believe in, and I already gave Gillian my word."

"Ah, so you're one of those disgustingly honest and trustworthy types," Erin teased, riffling through her purse. "Well, don't tell anyone, but so am I. So, run through the drill on this thing again for me?" Erin found the lipstick she was looking for and began to apply it, using the mirror on the sun visor.

"This is the go-see," Emma explained. "That's model-speak for audition, basically. When I called Gillian this morning, she said that she and Flash will be choosing the models they want to use for the shoot."

"Was she disappointed that all your other friends were tied up?" Erin asked, dropping her lipstick back into her purse.

"It's hard to say," Emma replied, as she and Erin got out of the car and began to walk toward the inn. "Gillian is the type who sort of gushes dramatically about everything—in a nice kind of way."

Once inside the ornate lobby of the inn, the girls saw an aisle with a sign on it:

BEAUTIFUL AD CAMPAIGN

MODEL GO-SEE SESSION

LOBSTERMEN'S ROOM, 10:00 A.M.

"Lobstermen's Room?" Erin asked. "Not very promising." She turned to Emma, looking uncertain. "Do you think I look okay?"

Emma looked over Erin's outfit. She'd chosen a black miniskirt and a pink

T-shirt. Over the T-shirt she wore a loose-crocheted pink sweater. Pink lipstick complemented her fair skin, and black and pink heart-shaped earrings hung on her ears, peeking through her wild hair.

"I think you look wonderful," Emma said warmly.

Erin smiled gratefully. "Thanks, I needed that. You're not so bad yourself, by the way!"

Emma looked down at her white linen pants and white vest over a sleeveless white lace T-shirt. "Somehow when I think about standing there in front of Flash, I wish I was wearing a paper bag."

Erin put her arm around Emma. "Don't worry," she said in a gruff, low voice, "I'll protect you!"

"My hero!" Emma trilled with a laugh, and they both headed for the Lobstermen's Room.

Emma kept a confident smile on her face as they walked along. *I wish I actually felt confident,* she thought anxiously, *but I don't. Not about Erin and not about myself. I'm afraid Flash will say something to totally humiliate me, and I'm afraid that he'll insult Erin.*

"Well, here goes," Emma said when they reached the door of the reception room.

"Wait a second," Erin said, putting her hand on Emma's arm. "Suddenly I am scared to death. Are you sure I should be doing this?"

"Of course!" Emma said emphatically.

"I'm not exactly a size six," Erin said. "And I'm not the kind of person who sets myself up for humiliation and failure, either."

"Listen, you look terrific," Emma insisted. "And Gillian was very clear about wanting to see all different types of beauty for this go-see. So you don't have anything to worry about."

Erin took a deep breath and let it out. "Okay," she said with finality. "I can handle it. Lead on!"

"That's the spirit!" Emma cheered, and she pulled open the door to the reception room.

"Come right on in, girls!" came Flash's familiar voice.

Emma's heart sank. She forced herself to plaster her most meaningless smile on her face and walk slowly into the room.

"Well, hit me with a hot note and knock me out!" cried Flash. "If it isn't Princess Grace herself!"

"Hello, Flash," Emma managed in an even voice.

122

"And a major hello right back atcha!" Flash said. He looked Emma up and down. "I gotta tell ya, honey, you still don't look like you sweat in the clinch, if you catch my drift!"

Emma's stomach churned. *Well, he hasn't changed a bit. He's using the same vacuous, sexist lines, and he looks the same, too. More gold jewelry than you could find on a rich sheik from Kuwait. White silk shirt unbuttoned down to his navel. Too-tight, too-new jeans tucked into black Italian boots. And that hair! He looks even sleazier with it slicked back like that. He's just all-around awful.*

"No, Flash, I don't catch your drift," Emma replied in an icy voice. "I never did."

"Ha!" Flash barked. "You kill me! Hey, you remember Leonard, my assistant, right?"

Standing next to Flash was his short, chubby, blond assistant, Leonard Fuller, whom Emma remembered as being perhaps the worst dancer she'd ever seen on the floor at a party. Emma realized that since she'd last seen Leonard, he'd grown a short ponytail and bought himself dark wraparound sunglasses that he was wearing now even though he was indoors.

"Hiya, Emma, remember me?" Leonard

called. "Maybe we can go dancing sometime!"

Emma smiled and kept her mouth shut.

"You remember that time you and me went dancing?" Leonard pressed. "I'm totally awesome!"

"As I recall, we didn't go out dancing," Emma said in a polite voice. "We danced together one time at a party."

"And it was unforgettable, am I right?" Leonard asked expectantly.

"Unforgettable," Emma agreed.

"I almost got picked for this MTV thing," Leonard went on, "you know, a music video kind of show, but they said I had too much style."

"I imagine so," Emma managed to say.

"Leonard, I need you to help me with something," Flash said, snapping his fingers at his underling. "Catch you later, princess," he added to Emma with a wink. Leonard hurried off after Flash.

"Oh, my God," Erin whispered to Emma, "Flash is even worse than you told me! Those guys need civilization lessons bigtime."

"No kidding," Emma groaned. "Sorry I convinced you to come along."

"No need to apologize," Erin said, grinning. "I'll just pretend it's a trip to the zoo!"

Emma looked around and noticed that there were already about forty girls in the room. Many of them were wearing something short or sexy—one was in a body-hugging Lycra catsuit, despite what Emma was sure were Gillian's clear instructions to the contrary—to "come as you are."

"I love my job!" Flash chortled to Leonard from across the room, indicating with his hands the group of women assembled for the go-see.

"Me, too, boss," Leonard said sychophantically, an eager grin on his face.

"Flash?" Emma asked, walking over to him.

"Hey, the heiress wants to ask me a question!" Flash exclaimed, as he checked one of his cameras. "Well, okay, babe, I will marry you, since you insist!"

Leonard laughed hysterically. "Boss, you kill me!"

"Is Gillian around?" Emma queried, ignoring Flash's terrible joke. "Because we're supposed to start at ten."

"And so we are, princess!" Flash agreed with her. "Gillian's run into town for something or other. She asked me to make the first cut."

Oh, great, Emma thought. *Gillian trusts*

this guy. She must not know anything about him, really.

"She asked *us*," Leonard said, winking at Flash, horning in on the conversation.

"Leonard, give it a rest." Flash glared at his assistant.

"Sorry, boss," Leonard said, chagrined.

"But we know you're already in, princess," Flash continued confidentially. "Gillian gave me the word. Besides, we already know ice doesn't melt under those hot kleig lights!"

"My name is Emma," Emma replied, with all the dignity she could muster.

"Sure thing, princess." Flash grinned.

Emma winced and glanced over at Erin, expecting to see a look of disgust on her friend's face. But Erin was only grinning. Clearly, she found Flash Hathaway and his sidekick, Leonard, totally hilarious.

"Hey, No-Sweat Cresswell," Flash continued. "You bring your good friend Big Red? You know, the one with the hoot-free hooters?"

"Big Red?" Erin echoed to Emma.

"Sam," Emma translated. "That's his idea of a clever nickname." She turned to Flash. "Sam had to work today."

"What about that other one?" Flash asked, a lecherous gleam in his eye. "You know, the brainy one with the Marilyn Monroe kinda curves—what's her name again?"

"Carrie," Emma said patiently.

"Yeah, Carrie," Flash recalled. "Her face was kinda ho-hum, but the bod was a major event, you know what I mean?"

Emma turned to Erin. "I don't think I can take this," she muttered.

"Oh, come on, he's a hoot!" Erin exclaimed. "You can't possibly take him seriously!"

"You're right," Emma agreed. "Okay. I can handle this." She spotted a small buffet table that had been set up along one wall. Suddenly, she got an uncharacteristic longing for a cream-filled doughnut. "Come on, Erin, let's go get a doughnut."

"Sounds good to me," Erin agreed.

"Yo, you with the big hair!" Flash yelled.

Erin turned around. "Me?"

"What's your name, sweetheart?"

"Erin. Erin Kane."

"Well, Erin, babe, your face won't break any mirrors, but you need a donut like you need a hole in the head, if you want my humble professional opinion."

"Gee, Flash, I really don't," Erin said earnestly.

Flash grinned. "Hey, Princess Grace

musta told you my name! She's so hot for me she can barely keep her hands off me, you know. She wants to do me bad."

"I'm going to vomit," Emma muttered. "I'm actually going to vomit."

"The reason that I knew your name is because it's on your name tag, big guy," Erin informed Flash.

Flash laughed. *It's impossible to insult him,* Emma thought to herself.

"You're quite the feisty one, huh, babe?" Flash asked Erin. He looked her over. "You're big, but you're curvy. It almost, kinda works. What do you weigh in at— two bills or so? If you don't mind my asking."

"I mind," Erin said, turning red with embarrassment. She turned on her heel and half-dragged Emma to the buffet. "I'd like to take that cream doughnut and smash it in his insipid face," Erin seethed.

"Well, as you can see, it's not so easy to laugh at him when he turns his charm on you," Emma pointed out.

"You're right," Erin agreed, pouring herself a cup of coffee. She edged past a beautiful African-American girl in tiny cutoff jeans and a lace top and looked around the room. The crowd had grown to maybe fifty or sixty girls. "There are a lot of gorgeous girls here."

Emma looked around the room. "I know," she agreed. "This kind of thing makes me feel so insecure."

"You?" Erin asked, looking surprised.

"Me," Emma insisted. "I feel as if I—"

"Oh, no," Erin groaned. "Look who just walked in the door."

Diana De Witt. Emma closed her eyes. *I wish I was any place except here,* she thought to herself. She opened her eyes. Diana was slowly moving into the room. She had on a low-cut black leotard with worn jeans, and she looked fabulous.

"She's spotted us and she's coming this way," Erin murmured. "Got a gun handy so I can shoot to kill?"

"Well, well, well, look who's here," Diana purred. "Is this some kind of a joke?"

"Could you please just go away?" Emma said coolly. "You don't like us and we don't like you, so what is the point of our carrying on a conversation?"

Diana laughed nastily. "Emma, dear, the truth of the matter is no one likes you. They're just too kind to tell you so to your face." She turned her gaze on Erin. "Are you here as Emma's cheerleader, or what?"

"I'm here on the go-see, the same as you," Erin managed in a steady voice.

Diana threw her head back and laughed. "You're kidding, of course."

"No," Erin said simply. "I'm not."

Diana sighed and shook her head sadly. "You must be totally delusional. Why don't you go suck up a rice cake, or something?"

"You know, your cruelty is truly ugly," Erin said, trying not to let her voice quake. "It's like you attack people so you can't be attacked, or something. What are you so afraid of that you have to leave packages with firecrackers on somebody's driveway?"

"Please," Diana scoffed. "You sound like something off of *Oprah*."

"Don't you even care if you hurt people?" Erin pressed. "Don't you know what it feels like?"

Diana's face hardened. "I don't let anyone hurt me, get it?"

"Well, someone must have really hurt you badly for you to have such a need to be so rotten," Erin said. "I feel sorry for you."

"*You* feel sorry for *me*?" Diana echoed stridently. "Now, that's rich. Just do me a favor, tubbo, and stay the hell out of my way." She turned on her heel and headed to the other side of the room.

"That was fabulous!" Emma cried, grabbing Erin's arm. "You really hit a nerve with her!"

"I didn't feel fabulous," Erin replied. "I felt like crying. I will just never understand what makes people like that tick."

"Maybe it has something to do with—" Emma began.

A piercing whistle screeched through the reception hall, stopping all motion and all conversation. Everyone turned in the direction of the whistle.

"Attention, attention!" Leonard Fuller's voice boomed out through the room. He was holding a microphone attached to a small portable sound system. "All models please sit in the holding area."

"What is a 'holding area?'" Erin asked.

"That," Emma replied, cocking her head toward an area that had been marked off with velvet ropes and contained rows of folding chairs. Together with the other girls, who apparently had been sent by various agencies at Gillian's request, Erin and Emma took a seat.

Flash and Leonard walked over toward them. Flash took the mike from Leonard.

"I love my job," he said to Leonard, not yet speaking into the mike. Then he turned to the group of models.

131

"I'm Flash Hathaway," he said. "You know why I'm here, and why you're here. We're gonna be choosing maybe eight, ten babes for this shoot. By Leonard's count, there are sixty-three of you here, which means the odds ain't good, but hey, that's show biz."

"Very encouraging," Erin whispered to Emma.

"He's a total creep," Emma observed.

"Leonard," Flash said, turning to his assistant, "crank up the music. It's magic time! We're gonna see how you move, see how you shake, see what kind of photos you take! God, I love my job."

"Excuse me," a girl in a long denim dress said, standing up. "But what does our dancing have to do with a print ad for rheumatoid arthritis?"

"I'm looking for fluid grace," Flash explained. "Besides, if *Beautiful* magazine decides to do the same ad for TV as a public service announcement, we're gonna show the babes actually moving. You gotta problem with that?"

"Yes, frankly, I do," the young woman said evenly. "It seems gratuitous and sexist."

"Yeah, I know what you mean," Flash said with a grin. He turned to Leonard.

"Okay, crank up the tunes. It's time to watch these girls boogie!"

"I can't believe it," Erin said to Emma. "He doesn't even care!"

On cue, Leonard ran over to a table with a CD player, and a couple of small speakers. He punched a button, and the sounds of Janet Jackson began to echo through the room.

"Okay, babes," Flash cried playfully. "Go for it!"

The girls all looked at each other. No one moved to get up to dance. Then a few of the girls rose, moved into the center of the room, and started dancing energetically to the music. Leonard boogied by himself in the corner, missing the beat completely, and Flash watched the four dancing girls through the viewfinder on his camera.

"Yeah, girls, shake that thang!" Flash crowed.

"This is totally demeaning!" Emma observed.

"I'm not doing it," Erin said, folding her arms.

Only four girls were dancing. Others were mumbling to each other. Even Diana was sitting with her arms folded, refusing to move. Some girls got up, ready to walk out in disgust.

"Do we stay here or do we leave?" Erin asked Emma over the blaring music.

Just then the power went off in the room. The music cut out, and the room went dark, except for the daylight that streamed through the windows. Everyone stopped what they were doing, as if they were a group of kids playing freeze-tag.

"What the hell is going on here?" shouted an Australian-accented voice. It was Gillian Garrett, dressed in a pair of black jeans and T-shirt that read "FIGHTING R.A. IS BEAUTIFUL," standing at the entrance to the room.

"We, uh, decided to get started without you," Flash said ingratiatingly.

"Why were these girls dancing?!" Gillian demanded, striding purposefully into the room.

"They wanted to warm up!" Flash defended himself. "It was chilly in here."

"He's lying," Erin said in a loud voice. "He told us to dance."

Flash shot Erin a dirty look.

Gillian turned to Flash, her eyes narrowing. He grinned and shrugged. "Well, I thought it might make them more comfortable, know what I mean? Everyone feels looser when they dance!"

Gillian turned away from Flash. "The

dancing is not necessary," she said in biting tones. "Now, everyone sit down, please. I'm not going to keep you here long. Let's pick the models and get you on your way. In case your agency didn't tell you the fee for this, it's one hundred dollars per model. I know the fee is low, but it's for a good cause, and many of us are working on this for free."

Erin turned to Emma. "You think I just blew my chance by ratting on Flash?"

"I think Gillian will like you better for it," Emma replied.

Erin's confidence seemed to be fading. She pulled nervously on the hem of her pink sweater. "I wouldn't care so much, except I really could use that hundred dollars."

"I think you've got a great chance," Emma assured her. But inside, she was a lot less confident. In fact, she was not very confident at all.

NINE

"This is so cool!" Erin whispered to Emma, a happy grin on her face. "I can't believe I got picked!"

"And Diana didn't!" Emma added, grinning back at Erin.

Thank goodness! Emma added to herself. *She's in! Gillian actually picked Erin to be in the advertisement. And Diana got eliminated. The look on her face when Gillian told her she could leave was priceless!*

It had actually come right down to the wire—Gillian had selected six other girls for the advertisement in addition to Emma, whom she had already chosen. They were all beautiful, though they were mixed in terms of type, age, and ethnicity. One thing Emma noticed, though, was that they were all either slender or average in weight. Then Gillian had looked over the remaining models, and Diana had even cleared her throat loudly to draw more attention to herself. But Gillian's eye slid right past her and rested on Erin. And that was that.

After dismissing all the other disappointed girls, she turned back to the group of models to give them her instructions. As she talked, Flash stood by her side. And rather than show any contrition for the dance stunt he'd pulled earlier, he wore that same I-got-away-with-something smile on his face.

"You're all to meet tomorrow morning," Gillian continued, "in the lobby of this inn. We'll bus you to the shoot site."

"Where's that?" one of the girls asked.

"North side of the island," Gillian responded. "At the beach house of *Beautiful*'s editor-in-chief and on the beach itself. Please bring summer sportswear—bathing suits, shorts, that kind of thing."

As Emma and Erin were leaving, Erin turned to Emma anxiously. "You don't think she'll expect me to pose in a bathing suit, do you?"

"I honestly don't know," Emma replied as they walked out the front door of the inn.

"You know, no matter how confident a

person you are, sometimes it's an uphill battle to not let insecurity kind of overwhelm you sometimes," Erin said with a sigh.

"I totally agree," Emma said. They walked to the Hewitts's car. "I don't believe it! Someone scribbled graffiti on the windshield!" Emma cried.

The two girls walked closer. Scrawled on the windshield in bright red lipstick was this message:

THE PRINCESS + THE PIG = TRUE LOVE

"Diana," Emma said in a low voice.

Tears came to Erin's eyes. "I don't know how much more of this I can take."

"She's getting worse and worse," Emma said. She turned to Erin. "I'm really sorry. If you weren't friends with me, you probably wouldn't be in for all this grief."

Erin swiped quickly at her eyes as they got into the car. "I can't believe I'm letting her get to me. It's not just her, I suppose. It's my dad losing his job, and money problems, and breaking up with my cheating boyfriend, and moving, and . . . just everything!"

"You feel kind of overwhelmed, huh?" Emma commiserated.

Erin nodded glumly. "I'll get over it," she assured Emma, searching in her purse for a tissue. "I take life seriously, but I don't take taking life seriously very seriously, if you know what I mean."

Emma laughed. "I do." Erin handed Emma a tissue, and Emma got back out of the car and wiped the windshield. All it did was smear the lipstick around.

"We could have Diana arrested for vandalism," Erin suggested.

"Not even worth the trouble," Emma replied. She opened the glove compartment and found a bottle of windshield cleaner. "Bingo! I'm lucky that the Hewitts are so organized."

Halfway to Erin's house, Emma turned to her. "You know, I'm serious about this perfume thing with your dad."

"Are you?"

Emma nodded. "I have all these plans for the future—like I really want to join the Peace Corps, for example. But they won't accept me until I've had more college. It seems like I spend all my time thinking about Kurt, crying about what went wrong, dreaming about things that will never be." She stopped at a red light. "Sometimes it feels like my entire life is on hold."

"But . . . why perfume?" Erin asked.

Emma shrugged. "I really like your father. And I think he got a rotten deal. And . . . maybe this is something concrete I can do to help, and something that will get my mind off myself at the same time."

Emma pulled the car into Erin's driveway.

"So, you want Dad to get you some facts and figures on what it would take to create a perfume and sell it here on the island?" Erin asked Emma.

"Yeah, I do," Emma replied.

Erin grinned at Emma. "You are one cool girl, Emma Cresswell," she said.

"Funny," Emma said simply, "I was just thinking the same thing about you."

"The bitch," Sam exclaimed, after Emma told her what Diana had done, "I would have gone after her and decked her." She reached for a nacho on the plate in the center of the table and bit into one hard.

"I thought about it," Emma said truthfully, as she chewed thoughtfully on a piece of celery, "but Erin was pretty upset."

"You guys need anything?" asked a waitress whom none of the girls recognized.

Sam, Emma, and Carrie looked at each other, and then all shook their heads.

"Okay," the waitress said, "I'll check back with you guys later. I can't guarantee when. It's a zoo in here tonight."

Emma, Sam, and Carrie had all met up at the Play Café for a late snack. It was already nearly midnight, but the café was as jammed as ever.

"I can't stay too long," Emma remarked. "I've got to be at the inn tomorrow morning by ten."

"You gotta hang for a bit," Sam protested. "Pres is coming over with Billy. Ah, yes, Presley my darling, this one is for you." She lifted up a nacho and gave it a warm kiss before putting it in her mouth and nibbling on it sensuously.

"Sam," Carrie commented, "that is repulsive."

"To know me is to love me," Sam sang out.

"I think it's great that Erin got picked for the modeling job," Carrie said. "I hope Diana didn't bum her out too much."

"Nothing keeps Erin down for long," Emma assured her.

"Good," Carrie said, sipping her diet Coke. "I really like her."

"Me, too," Sam said in agreement. "But, you know . . ."

"What?" Carrie asked her, reaching for one of the few nachos that Sam hadn't consumed.

"Well, I know we've talked about this before, but if Erin were to lose about forty pounds," Sam maintained, "Diana would have nothing to put her down about."

"Oh, come on!" Carrie exclaimed. "She'd just find something else!"

"Carrie's right," Emma agreed.

"Maybe," Sam said, "but Erin makes herself a walking target. Anyway, if she wasn't embarrassed about her weight, she wouldn't have gotten so upset at what Diana said."

"I can't believe you're saying that!" Carrie protested. "Diana humiliated her in front of everyone!"

"Well, that's exactly my point!" Sam replied.

"I remember a couple of times when Diana and Lorell made some comments about your bustline," Emma reminded Sam.

Sam looked down at her shirt. "What bustline?" she asked facetiously.

"It's easy to make jokes when you're here with Carrie and me," Emma said, "but you

143

were very upset and embarrassed at the time."

"Emma's right," Carrie said. "I remember."

"Me, too," Sam agreed a little sheepishly, reaching for the last nacho on the plate and popping it into her mouth. She chewed it thoughtfully. "But there's still a difference," Sam added.

"What's that?" Carrie asked.

"I can't do anything about my breasts, or should I say lack thereof," Sam countered.

"And you think Erin can lose weight if she really wants to," Emma surmised.

"Right," Sam agreed.

"Well, what if she's tried over and over again?" Emma asked.

"Then she should try harder," Sam said, holding her ground.

"And what if she's trying as hard as she can?" Emma queried.

"And what if she's happy the way she is?" Carrie asked. "I mean, society says we have this certain standard of beauty based on being thin. But at the turn of the century, society had a totally different standard. Erin would have been considered perfect, and everyone would be saying you weren't trying hard enough to gain weight!" Carrie told Sam.

Sam looked at Emma. "Is that true?" she asked doubtfully.

"It's true," Emma confirmed.

"I'm just so sick of this whole thin thing!" Carrie cried. "I know how hard it's been for me—I made myself sick over it at school! I mean, it's not like it's really important!"

Everyone was quiet for a moment after Carrie's outburst.

"Why does it feel so important then?" Sam asked.

No one had an answer. All three of them sat there thinking, while the Red Hot Chili Peppers blared out of the overhead speakers. Billy and Pres came pushing through the dense crowd over to their table.

"Hey," Pres drawled, "why so silent?" He slid in next to Sam and gave her a warm hug and kiss. Billy did the same with Carrie.

"You know, call me crazy but I kind of like you," Sam teased Pres.

"I already know you're crazy, girl," Pres said, nuzzling Sam's neck.

"I missed you, baby," Billy murmured to Carrie, but Emma overheard.

Well, I feel totally left out here, she thought to herself. *It wasn't like this when Kurt and I were together. God, I have to stop thinking about him. I just have to!*

"So," Pres drawled again, "were you talkin' about the future of the world, or what?"

"No," Emma spoke up, wondering why she was being so bold. "We were actually talking about Erin."

"Her weight," Sam said directly.

"What about it?" Billy asked with a shrug. "She's overweight. No big deal."

"I kind of have a thing for skinny women, myself," Pres said, tickling Sam.

"Oh, thanks a lot—" Sam protested.

"Seriously," Pres said, "Erin's real attractive. I can tell you for sure Jake thinks so." Pres looked around. "Say, do you think I could get a waitress's attention and get me something to drink?" He raised his arm to try to get served, but the café was so packed that no one saw him. He shrugged and reached over and took a sip of Sam's Coke.

"You really think Erin's cute?" Sam asked, astonished.

"Yeah, I do," Pres said. "And Jake thinks she's a stone fox."

"You mean you'd go out with her?" Sam pressed.

"I might," Pres allowed. "But of course, I got this fine redhead on my arm here, so I'm not looking."

"That was the right answer," Sam told him with a grin.

"You got me just in time," Pres joshed her.

Emma could see by the look in her friend's eyes that what Pres had said about Erin had really affected Sam. *It really means something to her that a guy as gorgeous as Pres is attracted to Erin,* Emma realized. *Now, why is it that we think we're worth more if guys think we're good looking? It's completely crazy!*

"So, what's this Carrie tells me about you guys going into business with Erin's dad?" Billy asked.

"Sam told me, too," Pres added. "Are ya'll really gonna do this thing?"

"We just might," Emma reported. "Mr. Kane is getting me some concrete information. When I dropped Erin off today, he gave me some pamphlets to read about perfume. I already gave them to Sam and Carrie."

"And we committed it all to memory," Sam reported, "because we are so brilliant."

"We learned about topnotes, middle notes, and dry downs," Carrie explained. "I never knew perfume was so complicated."

"Sounds musical," Pres mused.

"Think of it as music for your sense of smell," Emma said.

"Very poetic—I'm impressed!" Billy said with a laugh. "Now, would you like to translate that into English?"

"The topnote," Emma began, "is the first scent you get when you put perfume on your skin. It wears off pretty quickly."

"Then, after the perfume has been on for a few minutes, you get the middle note," Sam continued.

"And after it's been on a while, you get the dry down—that's the scent that stays with you," Carrie concluded.

"I really am impressed," Billy said again, smiling.

"Me, too," Pres commented. "So, are ya'll going to have time to do this perfume thing and do the band, too?"

"Never fear," Sam told him, "we will always have time for the Flirts."

"Speaking of which, we've got our first rehearsal with Erin this Saturday afternoon," Billy said.

"Sounds good to me," Sam said.

"Fine," Emma agreed.

"Can I shoot some pictures?" Carrie asked, sipping the last of her diet Coke. "You know, immortalize your first rehearsal together kind of thing?"

Billy leaned over and kissed her. "I always want you around, so it's cool with me."

Pres twirled a strand of Sam's hair around his finger, and Billy nuzzled Carrie.

Even in the midst of all her best friends, Emma suddenly felt very, very alone.

TEN

"Okay," Gillian yelled, her hands cupped
to her mouth, "let's call it a day, mates. It's
a wrap!"

"Thank God," Erin said to Emma, who
was standing next to her on the beach. "I
had no idea modeling was such hard work."

It was the morning of the *Beautiful*
photo shoot, and the fickle Maine weather
had changed again, turning hot and muggy.
Emma had been posing in her white-and-
navy–striped two-piece bathing suit, and
Erin had on white biker shorts with an
oversized multipastel-colored T-shirt, and
they were both sweating profusely. Flash
had had all eight models pose on the back
porch of the beach house, then on the
beach, then in the water, then pretending
they were playing volleyball on the beach.
The shoot seemed to go on and on. Every
few minutes, the makeup artist would run

over and powder the girls' faces again, and the hairdresser would try to fluff up hair that had become matted with sweat and sea air.

Even Flash seemed to feel the heat and the humidity. He called out his usual "Say cheese, babes," without his normal enthusiasm, and he'd insisted that instead of the usual rock and roll, cool jazz be played through the boom box he'd brought along to keep himself entertained as he worked.

"Don't forget, loves," Gillian reminded everyone, as they walked to the house from the beach, "to come over here and sign out. And to get your checks. You've certainly earned them."

"My check," Erin said, as she and Emma walked together toward the sign-out area. "I love the sound of that."

"Excuse me, Erin," Gillian called out.

"Yes?" Erin asked, turning to her.

"You did very well today, darling. I'm glad I picked you."

"Thanks!" Erin exclaimed. "I'm glad you picked me, too! Although I have to admit I never thought of myself as a model."

Gillian narrowed her eyes. "Actually, full-figured models are quite the rage now. You're a good size, in proportion, with a lovely face. And it just so happens, I'm about to open a full-figured division of my agency. Are you interested?"

"You're kidding," Erin said faintly.

"I'm quite serious," Gillian replied.

"Well, I . . . I don't know," Erin stammered. "I mean, I never thought about it. . . ."

"So now you'll think about it," Gillian said lightly. "Call my office in New York next week and we'll chat further, darling."

After Gillian had walked away, Erin turned to Emma. "Did you hear that?"

Emma nodded. "It's wonderful!"

"She's really serious?"

"Of course!" Emma insisted. The two girls walked over to the table to sign out. "Maybe this is the way you could make money for college."

"But . . . wouldn't I have to go to New York?" Erin wondered. "And if I did that, it would be so expensive I'd end up spending all the money I made, so it would be a wash."

"Well, I still think you should call Gillian," Emma said. "Hear her out."

They both signed out and were handed their paychecks by an assistant.

Erin made a smacking noise as she kissed the check. "I can really use this."

"Oh, Emma," Gillian called, hurrying

over. "I just wanted to remind you not to mention to Liz what I told you on the phone."

About my aunt being diagnosed with rheumatoid arthritis, Emma recalled. *I just can't believe Aunt Liz hadn't told me herself!*

"I'm worried about her," Emma admitted.

"I understand," Gillian commiserated. "But, darling, she has to handle it in her own way. I'm afraid I'm just shameless enough to have used the info to get you to agree to do this photo shoot. You really could make money modeling, you know."

Emma smiled. "But Gillian, I don't need any money."

Gillian shook her head ruefully. "Yes, unfortunately that particular lure doesn't work on you." She turned to Erin, wiping her perspiring forehead with a lace handkerchief. "Listen, I really do think you have a wonderful look."

"Thanks," Erin said.

"No, really love," Gillian said. "That amazing hair! And all those curves. We could make a lot of money together."

Erin grinned. "That lure may not work on Emma, but it *definitely* works on me."

"Gillian, here's my check," Emma said,

handing the envelope to her. "As I said, I'm not taking any money for this."

"Darling, they made out checks for everyone," Gillian explained. "Give the money to your favorite charity if you don't want it."

Emma patted the envelope thoughtfully. *I don't know what I'm going to do with it,* Emma thought to herself. *Probably give it to COPE, the Citizens of Positive Ethics here on Sunset Island. Kurt and I did so much good work for them before . . . Oh, no, there I go again, thinking about Kurt. Can't I just put him out of my mind?*

"Well, thanks again, girls," Gillian said, kissing both of them on both cheeks. "We'll be in touch!" she added before hurrying off.

"I don't know about you, but I need a very tall glass of iced tea," Emma said. "Want to go get one at the Play Café?"

"What?" Erin asked. "And leave before we say good-bye to Flash and Leonard?"

"I know it's rude, but let's risk it," Emma said dryly. "I'll be sure to write him a very well-bred thank-you note instead!"

After stopping for cold drinks, Emma dropped Erin off at her house, then headed back to the Hewitts's. Jane and Jeff were getting ready to go over to the country club for a family softball game at the day camp where Ethan was a counselor-in-training. Emma was staying home to care for Katie, who had the sniffles and didn't feel like going out.

"I can't tell you how much I'm looking forward to this," Jeff said sarcastically. "Broiling out there all alone in right field."

"I'll be right out there, broiling with you in left field," Jane reminded him. "Ah, the things we do for our kids!"

Jane pulled on a Boston University baseball cap and turned to Emma. "If we're not back by four o'clock, send out an ambulance equipped to handle heat exhaustion."

"Oh, by the way," Jeff added, "your friend Erin's dad stopped by and dropped off a large envelope for you. It's on the table in the hall."

After her parents left, Katie took a nap, during which Emma got to look at what Mr. Kane had brought over for her. It was detailed facts and figures, with estimates on what it would cost to create, manufacture, and then launch a perfume on Sunset Island. Emma was surprised to learn it wouldn't cost her all that much money as an initial investment. Before she could finish digesting all the information, Katie woke up. Emma gave her a snack and then watched a Disney video with her in the family room.

Emma sat on the couch with the little girl. Katie watched the cartoon, singing along with her favorite parts, and Emma went back to the data on the perfume, which she found completely fascinating. She was so engrossed, in fact, that she never heard the distant thunder, nor noticed the storm clouds building. Finally there was a clap of thunder loud enough to get her attention—and Katie's.

"My family is outside where they could get hurt," Katie said, looking worried.

"Don't worry, sweetie," Emma said, hugging the little girl. "They know enough to get in out of the rain."

Emma and Katie watched the storm as the rain pelted against the sliding glass doors. It wasn't long before the rest of Hewitts showed up, soaking wet.

Emma smiled. "Game called on account of rain?" she asked good-naturedly.

"Yep, and we almost got hit by lightning about a zillion times!" Wills said.

Jane grinned. "I think Wills is exaggerating slightly," she said. "But can you get us some towels?"

Emma rushed into the downstairs laundry closet and pulled out four or five towels, which she gave to each of the wet Hewitts. And by the time they had dried off a little, gone upstairs to change their clothes, and come back down, the rain had stopped and the sun was beginning to reappear.

"The weather has been just crazy lately," Jane commented. "Now it's sunny out."

"Great!" Ethan said. "We can start the game up again."

Jeff Hewitt shook his head. "I think the game's called off permanently," he commented. "But how about we order in some pizzas as a consolation prize? You hungry, Emma?"

"Actually," Emma said, in response to a sudden thought, "if it's okay with you, I'd like to go for a walk on the beach. I bet it's beautiful there now."

"It's fine with us," Jane said. "We're just going to hang out tonight and gorge ourselves on pizza and popcorn, which will be followed by hot fudge sundaes, if anyone has any room left—right kids?"

"Yeahhhh!" the kids cried.

Emma smiled, but that awful feeling clutched at her heart once more—that feeling of being all alone.

I was right, Emma said to herself, as she walked along the main beach of Sunset

Island. *It's absolutely magnificent out here now. Not to mention practically deserted. I definitely made the right decision.*

The beach was nearly empty—all the people having run for cover as the storm moved in. All that was left were a few people who had arrived at the end of the storm just as Emma had. And they were rewarded with cool breezes, rain-washed sand, and the remarkable sight of a thunderstorm moving east, out to sea. The only thing missing was a rainbow.

Emma walked along for a while, not thinking of anything in particular. Then for a time her thoughts focused on the perfume project. *We need a wonderful name,* Emma mused. *Mr. Kane says that the name has to capture the essence of the fragrance, and it's all-important to its success.*

She picked up a smooth stone and threw it out into the ocean. *This is the most beautiful place in the world,* she thought to herself. *It's so magical. Maybe we should name the perfume after the island. Sunset Island? No,* Emma thought, *that's not descriptive enough.*

What about Summer Storm? Or maybe Sunset something-or-other. . . . Emma thought. *No. Summer Storm doesn't work—at least I wouldn't buy a perfume with that name. Maybe the best thing to do is to try names out on Carrie and Sam together. Anything the three of us would all agree on would be perfect, wouldn't it? We're all so different from each other.*

Emma kept walking and thinking. As she neared the end of South Beach, she remembered the last time she'd been there with Kurt. *We were walking at the shoreline,* she remembered, *planning our future together.* A lump came to Emma's throat. It was almost as if she could see the two of them, hand in hand, back when they were so in love and everything wonderful still seemed possible.

And now it's all gone, Emma realized, tears coming to her eyes. *And I can never, ever go back.*

The beach was deserted now, and she was about to turn back when an eerie feeling came over her, as if someone were watching her.

She looked up, to the right, to the left. No one. But wait . . . Someone *was* watching her. He was standing on the rock jetty at the end of the beach, and he was staring right at her, his face set in hard lines of intense hatred.

Oh, my God, Emma thought, her heart

pounding in her chest, pure panic making her breath come hard and fast. *Oh, my God.*

It was Kurt.

ELEVEN

Kurt. The true love of her life. But no. It couldn't be. *I have to be seeing things,* Emma thought wildly. *Kurt is in Michigan with his cousin, and then he's going to Colorado. He said he could never face Sunset Island again after what happened between us. . . .*

Emma stood there transfixed in the late afternoon sunlight, her eyes magnetically locked on Kurt like a deer caught in the headlights of an oncoming car. He was staring right back at her, his expression grim.

Later, when Emma could reflect on those awful moments, she decided that it was like what people say happens when they're about to smash headlong into a tree, or when their plane is in trouble on a landing and they're skidding off the runway: their whole life passes before their eyes.

At that moment, in a heartbeat, Emma's whole life with Kurt Ackerman—her first true love—went rushing past her.

The first time I saw Kurt, my knees went weak, Emma remembered, as she stood there, frozen on the beach. *It was at the country club, last summer, and I'd brought Katie Hewitt there for her first swimming lesson. I thought Kurt was the most gorgeous guy I'd ever seen in my life. I was so shy I didn't even know how to talk to him—I sounded too proper and ridiculous.*

And our first date, when he took me to dinner at his adopted Aunt Rubie's restaurant, and afterward we walked on the beach . . . our first kiss . . . the first moment that I realized how special he is, how unique, the first moment I knew I could love him forever.

The images continued to whiz through Emma's mind. *There we are, together, raising money for COPE, going door to door trying to let people know that Sunset Island isn't perfect, that there are poor people who live here as well as the rich people, and that we're going to have to do something about it, even if the wealthy summer people would like it all swept under the rug.*

There's Kurt in jail for a crime he didn't commit, and me and Jane Hewitt going to visit him and bail him out. God, does he look exhausted!

And there we are together in the office of Sunset Travel on Main Street, planning our honeymoon. He's saying something ridiculous about bombing around Maine in a four-wheel drive truck for a couple of weeks. And I'm getting so mad at him. But am I really so mad at him, or at myself for agreeing to get married when I wasn't really ready? Why didn't I know the truth in time? Why did things have to end the way they did? How could I hurt him so horribly when I love him so much? Loved him so much? Oh, dear God, I still love him. What am I going to do?

As Emma stood there, frozen, unable to move, Kurt slowly walked over to her. She could feel her breath coming in short, shallow gasps. Still she couldn't move.

Kurt stood not five feet away from her now. *He's so beautiful,* she thought wistfully, *tall and handsome, with his light-brown, gold-streaked hair and a gorgeous face. He's still tan, and he looks like he's been working out.* But he looks so sad, Emma noted. *His eyes are filled with sorrow.*

It seemed like an eternity before either of them said or did anything.

"Emma," Kurt finally said in a low voice.

"Hi," Emma managed.

"I was hoping I'd never see you again."

It was like a punch in the stomach. All the air went out of her, leaving behind only a searing, gut-wrenching pain. "I understand that's how you feel," Emma finally managed to whisper. "I . . . I can't tell you how sorry I am that I hurt you. I never meant to."

Kurt managed a bitter smile. "I have no idea what that means, Emma. Are you telling me you aren't responsible for your own actions?"

"Yes, I'm responsible," Emma said, trying to keep her voice steady. "But I couldn't go through with it just to avoid hurting you. That would have hurt you even more."

"You thought about that just a little too late, didn't you?" Kurt asked sharply.

"Yes, I did," Emma agreed. "That's what I'm truly sorry for."

"Are you?" Kurt asked. "Well, what difference does it make anymore?"

He looked away, out to the sea, and Emma noticed again how very sad he looked. *I wish I could put my arms around him and make everything okay,* Emma thought sadly. *I wish there was some way he could know how much I still love him.*

But it's too late for us. I know it's too late.
He'll never be able to forgive me.

"What are you doing here?" Emma asked softly. "I thought you were in Michigan."

"I was," Kurt said. "But I came back." He stuffed his hands deep into the pockets of his worn jeans.

"Why?" Emma asked quietly.

"Why?" he echoed angrily. "Why? The last time I looked, I grew up on this island, and you're the rich girl from Boston who's making herself feel better by working here for the summer, even though she doesn't have to work a day in her life if she doesn't want to. That's why!"

Emma looked away, hurt. "That's not fair and you know it, Kurt." She looked back up at him to see if her words had any effect on him.

"Look, that isn't the point," Kurt said, running his fingers nervously through his hair. "I love this island. I grew up here. It's my island, not yours. And I'm damn well not going to let you run me off it."

"I never wanted you to leave the island," Emma said. "That was your choice."

He laughed, a short, angry sound. "My *choice*?" he exclaimed, his voice rising. "After you humiliated me in front of everyone I care about?"

167

"Don't yell at me," Emma told him quietly, desolation seeping into every pore. "Just say what you want to say. I can take it."

Kurt looked at her. "You humiliated me," he repeated in a low, angry voice. "Don't you ever have any regard for anyone else's feelings but your own?"

"I know how much I hurt you—"

"You keep saying that," Kurt interrupted, "but you really don't. You can't possibly know how it felt—how I feel."

"Maybe I can't," Emma agreed.

The two of them stood there together quietly. To Emma, the five feet separating them felt like five hundred miles. But at the same time, she felt an irrational urge to run to Kurt, to throw herself in his arms, to cry on his shoulder, and to feel Kurt's strong arms around her again as they'd been around her so many times before.

She could actually see herself doing it! She could practically feel Kurt comforting her, drying her tears, holding her close. . . .

But no. She would never, ever have that again.

"Why, Emma?" Kurt finally whispered, breaking the wall of silence. "Why did you do it?"

"I was stupid," Emma replied. "What else can I say?"

"You're right," Kurt agreed. "But I was stupid, too."

"You?" Emma asked in shock.

"Yeah, me," Kurt admitted. He turned away from her, looking out to the sea once more. Emma followed his gaze. There was a young couple walking arm in arm along the dunes, laughing, talking, stopping to hug and kiss, obviously in love.

I had that once, Emma thought. *With him. Now look at us!*

"I was stupid," Kurt repeated, turning back to Emma. "You think I couldn't see what was going on? What do you take me for, an idiot?"

"No—"

"I was a fool," Kurt insisted vehemently. "It was so obvious that you didn't want to marry me. Any idiot could have seen that."

"But I *did* want to marry you!" Emma exclaimed.

"Bull," Kurt barked.

"I did," Emma insisted. "I don't know how to explain. When you proposed and I said yes, I meant it with all my heart!"

"But you just kind of changed your mind, is that it?" Kurt asked. "No big deal, sorry, buddy, no hard feelings?"

"No, no, it wasn't like that at all!" Emma exclaimed wildly. Tears came to her eyes. She couldn't stop them. "I loved you more than I ever loved anyone in my life. But . . . I wasn't ready to get married!"

"You discovered that a little late, too, didn't you?" Kurt asked bitterly.

"Yes, I did," Emma agreed, the tears falling silently down her cheeks. "I should have known myself better than that, but I didn't. The truth is, I was afraid if I didn't marry you I'd lose you!" She was sobbing now, great wracking sobs that were tearing through her chest.

"Emma!" Kurt said gruffly. "You can't marry someone so you won't lose them!"

"I know that!" Emma cried, trying to stop her tears. "I was an idiot!" She turned away from him and wiped at her face, trying to get a hold of herself.

And then she felt his hand on her arm. Slowly, she turned around. They stood there, so close that she could feel his breath on her face. She looked up at him, the tears still pooled in her eyes, searching his face for forgiveness.

For a moment, the briefest moment, she thought he was going to kiss her. *Please, oh please kiss me,* she prayed. But just as it seemed that his lips were going to come down on hers, he took a step away from her and shoved his hands back into his pockets.

Emma took a deep breath and forced herself to regain control. "I'm sorry I lost it like that," she said.

"Forget it," Kurt mumbled.

"So, when did you come back?" Emma asked, forcing herself onto a more neutral topic.

"Yesterday," Kurt said, "to pick up my stuff and visit my father before school."

"School," Emma repeated faintly.

"I'm going to the Air Force Academy in the fall," he explained.

"I heard."

"Through the grapevine," Kurt observed wryly. "I can imagine what the grapevine is saying about me."

"They blame me," Emma said, "not you."

"They're right," Kurt commented.

"Yes, they're right," Emma agreed. "I totally messed up. I know that." She screwed up all her courage. "But, Kurt, you did, too."

"I can't believe you're saying that—"

"Just hear me out," Emma said, trying to sound mature and reasonable. "Wasn't one of the reasons you asked me to marry you because I said I was going to join the Peace Corps and you were afraid you'd lose me?"

"I asked you to marry me because I loved you—"

"And I loved you, too," Emma said passionately. "But tell the truth. You were afraid I'd go to Africa, and we'd lose each other. Just like I was afraid I'd lose you if I didn't marry you."

"It's not the same," Kurt maintained stubbornly. "You could have said no. I wouldn't have broken up with you."

"Maybe not," Emma said. "But I felt kind of pressured anyway. I thought that if I said no when you proposed, things would never be the same between us."

"Well, we'll never know now, will we?" Kurt asked.

"No, we never will."

A seagull shrieked overhead, and in the distance Emma could hear children laughing, a radio playing near the boardwalk, someone calling out to a friend.

So this is how it really ends, Emma thought, her heart filled with pain, *with all these ordinary sounds around me, with people going about their lives as if it were any other day. . . .*

"What do we do now?" Emma asked.

"We move on," Kurt said tersely. "What else can we do?"

Fall into each other's arms, that's what, Emma longed to say. *Admit that we made mistakes and start over. How can we just throw it all away? How?*

But she couldn't say it. She knew she had hurt him too deeply. He could never trust her again. "Yes, we just have to move on," Emma agreed.

"If only we could turn back time, huh?" Kurt said softly.

She looked at him with surprise, hope filling her heart. "Would you wish for that?"

He sighed. "I just don't know anymore." Kurt picked up a shell and threw it out to sea. "Sometimes when I can't sleep at night, I think about everything that happened with us—how jealous I got, how much I resented your having money, how stupid I was that time I slept with Diana . . . and then I wish I could kind of roll everything back to when we first met and fell in love. Sort of like a do-over in a kid's game," he added with a sad smile. "And maybe then everything would turn out differently."

"Don't you think . . . I mean, isn't

there any chance we could try again?" Emma asked.

He stared at her a moment. "No," he finally said. "That's not how life is, Em. We'd never be able to pretend all the stuff that's happened didn't happen."

"But—" she protested.

"That's just not the real world," Kurt continued. "We have to move on. All I know is that it really hurts to see you again. I just can't take this kind of pain."

"What does that mean, then?" Emma whispered, the tears springing to her eyes again.

"It means good-bye," Kurt said. "Forever. I never want to see you again."

"I understand," Emma managed to utter, turning away quickly so he wouldn't see the tears flooding her eyes. "Good-bye, Kurt," she said, her back to him, and then she began to walk away.

Please, please, please follow me, Emma thought desperately as she took her first few steps. But she heard no footsteps in the sand behind her.

Just as she reached the boardwalk, he called out her name.

"Emma!"

Emma turned quickly. He was standing in exactly the same spot she had left him.

"You know what I said to you," Kurt yelled, "about me never wanting to see you again?"

Emma nodded.

"I lied," Kurt shouted. "I lied!"

TWELVE

Emma ran back to the Hewitts's, hoping that the physical exercise would offer some release from her pain. It didn't work. She arrived back at the house panting hard and sobbing harder.

She found Erin sitting on the Hewitts's front porch.

"My God, what happened?" Erin asked her, jumping up quickly. "Are you okay?"

"I'm okay," Emma said, the tears coursing down her cheeks belying her words. She buried her head in her hands. "No, I'm not. Oh, God, I want to die!"

Erin put her arm around Emma and let her cry. "Do you want to talk about it?" she finally asked.

Slowly Emma told Erin the whole story, how she'd run out on her wedding to Kurt, and everything that had just happened when she'd run into him on the beach.

"What happened after he said he really did want to see you again?" Erin asked.

"He walked away," Emma said desolately. "He just . . . walked away!"

"But now you know he still cares," Erin pointed out gently.

"But he's leaving the island!" Emma cried. "I'll never see him again!"

Erin patted Emma's back softly. "I don't know what to say. . . ."

"There's nothing anyone can say," Emma said, taking the tissue Erin offered her. "God, I'm a wreck." She blew her nose a couple of times. "I just don't know how to get over this."

"Time?" Erin suggested.

"Yeah, that's what everyone says," Emma agreed. "But time keeps passing, and I still hurt just as much." She managed a watery smile. "I'm sorry to bore you with all this."

"It's not boring," Erin assured her. "We're friends, I hope."

"We are."

"Well, then, you'll just return the favor for me sometime." She lifted a large envelope. "I was on my way to meet Jake for dinner at the Play Café, and I thought I'd stop by with this stuff for you from my dad. It's more perfume information."

"Thanks," Emma said, taking the envelope. "I need to throw myself into this project and get my mind off Kurt."

"And maybe . . ." Erin began, "well, maybe you need to start dating again."

Emma shook her head. "I tried that. I'm just not ready."

Erin stood up and looked thoughtful. "Hey, do you have to work tonight?"

"No, the Hewitts's are having one of their family junk food dinners—pizza, popcorn, ice cream—I'm free to wallow in my misery."

"Why don't you come to dinner with me and Jake?" Erin suggested.

"No," Emma insisted. "You guys have a date."

"It's more casual than that," Erin assured her. "I'm taking it really slow with Jake. Please come. I want you to."

Emma looked skeptical. "Are you sure?"

"Absolutely," Erin said. "What would you do here, just go up to your room and cry some more?"

"Probably," Emma admitted. She blew her nose again. "If you're really sure—"

"Yes," Erin said firmly, reaching for Emma's hand to pull her to her feet. "Come on, I'll drive. And we won't talk about anything more serious than who's cuter—Johnny Depp or Joey Lawrence."

"Johnny Depp," Emma said, trying for some levity.

"I'd have to kiss both of them for long periods of time before I could fully judge," Erin said.

Emma got in the car and tried to smile. "I'll see what I can arrange."

"We're here before the crowds," Emma observed, as she and Erin walked into the half-full Play Café.

"Good," Erin said, looking around for Jake. "I'm not in the mood for major noise tonight. I guess we beat Jake here."

First Emma went to the ladies' room to wash her face and reapply some mascara and light lipstick, then the two girls headed back to the booth Emma always sat in with Sam and Carrie, and they slid into the seats.

"Does this place actually serve anything besides pizza, burgers, and nachos?" Erin asked Emma.

"They have salads," Emma said. "They're just not very good."

"I heard there's a really good seafood restaurant—" Erin began, but she was stopped by the feel of something pushing into her back.

"Hands up," a low male voice said.

It was Jake, with a water pistol. He winked at Emma.

Erin raised her hands. "If you're robbing me, buddy," she said jovially, obviously recognizing Jake's voice, "you're gonna be real disappointed. I've got about four bucks in my purse."

"Well, then, I'll just have to shoot you," Jake said. He came around the booth and shot his water gun at Erin. "Direct hit!" he yelled. "Five points!"

"Do you see the juvenile behavior I'm forced to put up with?" Erin asked Emma, wiping the water off her face.

Jake leaned over and kissed her, then he slid into the booth. "You look cute wet."

"Gee, thanks," Erin replied. "Where were you? We didn't see you when we came in."

"Back watching a pool game," Jake explained. "Some guy named Butchie Gleason is in a hot pool tournament back there. He already beat Pres and Billy."

"Butchie's really good," Emma said. "I hope the guys didn't bet a lot. Last summer he won a lot of money from a friend of ours, Howie Lawrence."

Jake grinned. "Actually, I think Butchie is just about to get his butt kicked. Carrie is playing him now."

"Carrie's here?" Emma asked quickly.

Jake nodded. "Sam, too."

"Carrie's a pool shark," Emma said. "She beat Butchie last year—he still hasn't lived it down."

"Well, I guess he's going for a rematch," Jake said. "You ought to go root for her."

"I think I will," Emma said eagerly, sliding across the booth. "Excuse me."

She hurried back to the pool table, where a small crowd surrounded the table.

"Yo, Emma!" Sam called when she saw her. "I didn't know you were here!"

"I came over with Erin," Emma explained. Carrie was busy lining up a shot, and hadn't noticed Emma yet. Emma looked over at the pool table, where four solid balls and two striped balls lay on the table, along with the black eight ball. "Who's winning?"

"Butchie, at the moment," Sam said. "He's stripes."

Carrie went for a side pocket shot. She hit the cue ball with her stick, and the cue ball hit a solid purple ball, which banked and then slid neatly into a side pocket. Carrie walked around the table, checking out her possibilities. She leaned over and quickly made another shot. A solid red ball slid into the front pocket.

"Is she cool or what?" Sam whispered to Emma.

There were two solid balls left on the table. Carrie proceeded to make both shots. Then she called the eight ball for the left side pocket, and she snapped it into the hole.

The group around the table began to applaud and whistle. Billy gave Carrie a big hug. Then Carrie turned around to Butchie and stuck out her hand. "It was a pleasure beating you again this year," she told him.

Butchie scowled and refused to shake Carrie's hand. "I'm gonna get you yet, babe," he sneered, and stomped out with his friends.

"Such bad manners," Sam chided. She picked up the money they had bet from the side of the pool table and handed it to Carrie. "All yours, sweet-ums!"

Carrie took the money, which Emma could see was six twenty-dollar bills. "I'm rich!" Carrie crowed.

"Does this mean you're taking me to dinner?" Billy asked her.

"This means I'm taking everyone to dinner!" Carrie exclaimed happily. Just then she noticed Emma. "Hi!" she said, giving Emma a hug. "When did you get here?"

"In time to see your spectacular finish," Emma said warmly.

"I may have to give up college and go on the pool circuit," Carrie mused.

"Your parents would kill you," Billy pointed out.

"That's true," Carrie admitted. "And it's so hard to play pool if you're dead. Hey, let's go get a big table and order tons of food. It's on me!"

"That's what I like—an exuberant and generous winner," Pres said with a grin.

"I was sitting with Erin and Jake," Emma explained.

"So, let's go get them," Carrie said. "It sounds like fun."

Emma smiled self-consciously. "Three couples and me?" she asked quietly.

"Oh, please, someone get me out a violin so I can play tragic music," Sam teased. "Em, get a grip. This is not three couples and you. This is you with all your best friends, get it?"

"Got it," Emma replied, trying to sound convinced.

They got Erin and Jake and moved to a round table where they could all fit.

"Hey, I love that outfit," Erin told Sam.

"It is cool, isn't it?" Sam said. She had on an antique white cotton slip, with eyelet lace around the neck and hemline, over a white baby's T-shirt. On her head she wore a black velvet beret with a silver heart-shaped broach pinned on it. Cream-colored ribbed leggings adorned her legs, and her usual red cowboy boots were on her feet. "I got the whole thing for about eight dollars at that used clothing store that just opened on the north side of the island," Sam explained. "It's called 'Kkool Junkk.' And guess who owns it? Kurt's Aunt Rubie's sister, Jade!"

Everyone got quiet at the table. They all knew she was referring to Kurt's adopted aunt, which meant that everyone was now thinking about Kurt.

"Oops," Sam said meekly. "I guess I shouldn't have mentioned that."

"It's okay," Emma said stoically.

"Well, well, well," came Diana's familiar ugly voice. "If it isn't all the Flirts, one big happy family." Diana sauntered over to their table, her friend Lorell trailing behind.

"Diana," Billy said jovially, "we were just celebrating having you out of the band."

Diana's eyes narrowed. "You'll live to regret it," she promised.

"What is your problem, girl?" Pres asked her. "I know it's obvious to you that we don't want you around. A person might just think you like being disliked."

Diana smiled coolly. "You know, cowboy, it may be hard for you to believe, but I don't spend any time worrying about any of you, one way or the other."

"Well, good," Sam said. "I am ever so relieved. Now, go away."

Diana's eyes flicked over the group, until they rested on Erin. "Oh, look who's become a big part of your group. And I do mean *big*." She looked over at Lorell. "This is the moose—I mean—the girl I told you about."

Lorell leaned forward. "Honey, don't you have any pride?" she asked Erin in her sickeningly sweet Georgia drawl. "How can you go around with all that fat on you? I could just cry for you, I really could!"

Erin blushed a deep red. "God, Diana, you actually have a friend who's just as cruel as you are. The two of you deserve each other!"

"Why, I was only trying to help!" Lorell insisted indignantly. "I know a wonderful fat doctor. He could suck some of that lard off you in nothin' flat!"

"Geez, what a pair," Jake mumbled, a look of disgust on his face.

"Some people just thrive on nastiness, I guess," Erin said, trying to look unaffected.

"Oh, that's not nasty," Diana said, shaking her curls off her face. "I mean, for example, it would be nasty to call you a fat slob in front of your friends, which you notice I didn't do. It would be nasty to—"

Emma was on her feet. "Diana!" she yelled. "You have been a bitch to me all my life, and now you're being a bitch to my friends. Well, I'm sick of it! And I'm not putting up with it anymore!"

Emma grabbed Jake's squirt gun out of his pocket and squirted Diana's face hard, over and over. Diana was so shocked she just stood there for a moment, her mascara making small rivers of black down her cheeks.

"Well, well, well, who would have thought you had any spunk in you," Diana finally managed. Lorell grabbed a napkin off a nearby table and quickly handed it to Diana, who began to wipe off her face.

"You don't know anything about me," Emma seethed. "You never did. Now get the hell away from here before I kick your ass out."

Emma's friends were in a state of shock. Emma had never spoken that way before in her entire life.

"Oh, I know more about you than you think," Diana said, trying to sound cool. "For example, I know that you saw Kurt today."

Emma could feel everyone's eyes on her. "How did you know that?" she asked in a low voice.

"Well, let's see," Diana mused, "could it be because he told me himself?"

Emma couldn't move.

"And I happen to know you begged him to take you back, and he never wants to see your lying little face again as long as he lives."

"That's not what happened—" Emma began

"Sure," Diana taunted her, feeling in charge again. "Well, when I'm in bed with him tonight—like I was last night—I'll be sure to tell him you said hello." She grinned evilly at Emma. "Who has the last laugh now, huh? Ha-ha-ha." She turned and walked away, Lorell trotting after her.

For a moment Emma was rooted to the spot. Then she swiftly strode across the café and spun Diana around by the shoulder. Then she lifted her right hand, pulled it back, and slapped Diana across the face as hard as she possibly could.

Diana shrieked and reached out for Emma, but Emma had already slipped out of her reach. Then she turned and marched back to her friends.

Diana was struggling with the bouncer by the door, who had moved in quickly and was now holding her arms. "I think you should just leave," he was saying to her. She finally broke free, screaming and cursing, and crashed out the door with Lorell.

Everyone at Emma's table applauded wildly.

"Dang if you don't pack a mean wallop!" Pres cheered.

"I can't believe it!" Sam yelled happily. "I never thought I'd live to see the day Emma Cresswell got into a brawl!" She jumped up and held Emma's hands over her head like a victorious prize fighter. "The winner and new world champion!"

Then Sam saw that tears were making rivers down Emma's cheeks. "Em?"

Emma turned and fled to the ladies'

room, sobbing her heart out. A couple of minutes later, Sam, Carrie and Erin pushed in through the door.

"Erin told us about you and Kurt," Carrie explained, putting her arms around Emma.

"My whole life is ruined!" Emma sobbed. "And now Kurt's back with Diana! I just can't stand it!"

"She's probably lying like she always does!" Sam exclaimed.

"Kurt and I were the only ones on the beach," Emma managed to gasp out between tears. "He's the only one who could have told her we saw each other."

"Okay," Carrie agreed, "but that doesn't mean he's really sleeping with her. I mean, she didn't get the story right about what went on between you and Kurt, did she?"

Emma shook her head no, and explained what had actually happened.

"Maybe you and Kurt will get back together," Erin ventured.

"It's too late," Emma cried. "He'll never forgive me and he'll never forget. You don't know him. And now he's probably sleeping with Diana again, like he did last summer!"

"I don't believe that," Carrie said staunchly.

Emma leaned her head back against the wall. "I just feel so . . . so awful! I can't stop thinking about him! I can't stop regretting what I did. And I can't stop myself from still being in love with him."

Sam handed her a box of tissues from the counter. Emma grabbed a handful. "I'm spending my life awash with tears," she said in a nasal voice, and blew her nose loudly. "You can all go back to your dates. I'm not exactly great company now."

"Yeah, like we'd really leave you here," Sam snorted. "Emma, you're my best friend, remember? If you hurt, I hurt."

"How about if we go out back and get a little air?" Carrie suggested.

"I'll stop by the table and tell the guys," Erin offered, hurrying out of the ladies' room.

They walked onto the back patio and down the steps that led to the beach. Emma stared out at the ocean. "Thanks for everything," she told her friends.

"All for one and one for all, you know our motto," Sam said.

"I really have to get my life back together," Emma said. She turned to Erin, who had returned from speaking to the guys. "Tell your dad the fragrance is a go," she said firmly.

"Are you sure this is a good time for you to make a decision like that?" Erin asked. "I mean, you're kind of distraught."

"It's a perfectly good time," Emma said, trying to sound strong. "I can't go on like this anymore. And I absolutely can't date anyone else yet." She looked over at Sam. "Not even Adam—it isn't fair to him."

Sam nodded with understanding.

Emma looked back out at the ocean. "I just know that . . . that I have to find some answers inside myself."

"You're a very strong person, Emma," Carrie said quietly. "You always have been."

"You think so?" Emma asked earnestly. "That's funny. I don't feel very strong." She reached down and picked up a handful of sand, which she let sift through her fingers. "Do you guys really want to go into business with me?"

"Are you kidding?" Sam asked. "Is the pope Catholic?"

"Carrie?" Emma asked.

Carrie smiled. "I think we'd be fabulous together."

"Erin?"

"Sorry," Erin said quickly. "I mean, my father is so excited that he paces the floor at night. But I have no mind for business at all. But if this thing ever gets off the ground, how about if I sing the jingle or something?"

"It's a deal," Emma agreed swiftly. "Between the Flirts and taking care of the Hewitt kids and this perfume business, I won't have any time to feel sorry for myself. I'm going to move on with my life. Just like Kurt is."

"You really will fall in love again one day," Carrie said quietly.

"Maybe," Emma whispered, gulping hard. "But it will never be quite the same, you know what I mean?"

There was no reply but the distant sound of a mournful gull, calling to his mate.

"Thanks for the ride," Emma told Erin, as she got out of Erin's car later that evening. "And thanks for being such a good friend."

"In the words of Sam," Erin said, "right back atcha." Erin leaned over the seat to see Emma better. "You okay?"

"Yes, I think I am," Emma said, her voice steady. "Tell your dad I'll call him tomorrow, okay?"

"Okay," Erin agreed. "He's going to be thrilled, Emma. You are doing a wonderful thing."

"I'm lucky to get to work with him," Emma replied. "Goodnight." She walked into the house and crept quietly up the stairs so she wouldn't wake any of the Hewitts. Quickly she washed her face and brushed her teeth, then she changed into the long T-shirt that she loved to sleep in.

She got into bed and closed her eyes, suddenly overwhelmed with exhaustion. So much had happened.

Carrie says I'm a strong person, Emma mused, turning over to snuggle into a better position. *I remember reading somewhere once that you can only learn through adversity. Well, if that's true, I must be getting really, really smart.*

She drifted off to sleep, her last thoughts of various names for their perfume, which she concentrated on to try to block out images of Kurt.

Ping! Ping! Ping!

She opened her eyes.

What was that?

Ping! Ping! Ping!

She heard it again. It was coming from the window. Emma sat up and padded across the room. She looked out the window, the yard illuminated by a full moon.

And standing there, throwing small rocks up at her window, was Kurt.

"Am I dreaming?" she asked herself out loud, and then she actually pinched herself to make sure this was really happening.

Quickly she opened the window and looked down at him. She didn't say a word. She couldn't.

"I didn't want to wake everyone," he whispered up to her.

Emma closed her eyes and remembered the first time Kurt had thrown rocks at her window. She'd run down to him, and he'd held her in his arms. It was the very first time he'd told her that he loved her.

"Can I talk to you for a minute?" Kurt whispered. "Can you come down?"

She hesitated, both scared and hopeful at the same time.

"It'll just be a minute, I promise," Kurt said.

She made a decision. Quickly she ran across her room, pulled open the door, and ran downstairs to him.

He looked at her in her T-shirt. "Aren't you cold?"

She shook her head, too paralyzed with

mixed emotions to feel much of anything in the way of temperature.

"I wanted to tell you," Kurt began, "I'm sorry I just left like that this afternoon."

"Why did you?" Emma asked.

"It's . . . tough to see you," Kurt admitted. "It's . . . it's painful."

"I understand," Emma said. She took a deep breath. "I saw Diana tonight. She said you two were seeing each other again."

"It's not true," Kurt said in a low voice. "I'm not in any shape to get involved with anyone right now." He ran his hand through his hair like he always did when he was nervous. "I ran into her this afternoon, and she asked me if I'd seen you, and I told her I had just seen you on the beach. That's about it."

Kurt looked up at the starry sky. "How did things get so screwed up for us, Em?"

"I don't know," Emma said. "We both made a lot of mistakes, I guess."

"Yeah," Kurt agreed, looking back at Emma.

Emma clenched her fists tight, said a swift prayer, and then uttered the most difficult words she had ever had to say. "Kurt," she said, "I know you can never forgive me for what I did, but I have to tell you this. I still love you."

He just stood there, staring at her.

"I love you," she repeated passionately. "I can't stop loving you. You're inside my heart, and no one else can get in."

"I love you, too," Kurt whispered, and by the light of the moon Emma could see tears streaming down his cheeks. "Don't you know that? Can't you tell? There's no one else like you, Emma. You're . . . you're magic. And what we had together was magic. I don't know if that ever happens twice in one person's life. Most people don't even get it once."

"Can't we try again?" Emma cried. "Can't we, please?"

"I don't know," Kurt said in a ragged voice. "I need some time alone. Time to think. Can you understand that?"

"Yes," Emma whispered. "I can."

And I really do, she realized. *As much as I want him to take me into his arms and say that everything is the way it was before, we can never go back. We can only go forward. And the only hope we have is to learn from our mistakes and try not to make the same mistakes again.*

"Can we write to each other?" Kurt asked softly.

"Yes," Emma replied in a steady voice. "I'd like that."

"I would, too," Kurt agreed. He managed a crooked grin. "Like I said, Emma, you're magic. And you can't just give up on magic, can you?" He put his hands deep in his pockets, smiled wistfully at her one more time, and then he disappeared into the night.

Emma sat on top of the picnic table, listening to Kurt's car starting up and pulling away from the house. She looked up at the stars. And in her heart was both a new strength and a tiny sliver of hope that hadn't been there before.

"Hey, all you stars," she called out softly. "I'm Emma Cresswell, and I'm magic!"

Could it be true? she wondered. *Can I possibly believe in myself enough to feel that special? With or without Kurt?*

"Well, stars," she whispered, "I can try. I can really, really try."

And then it came to her, and a grin spread across her face. She knew what the name of the perfume should be: Sunset Magic.

"Sunset Magic," she said out loud. It sounded perfect.

Just then, a shooting star darted across

the sky. She closed her eyes and made a wish, which she believed in her heart could come true, would come true.

Emma Cresswell believed in magic.

Introducing
Cherie Bennett's exciting new
series

CLUB SUNSET ISLAND

Turn the page
for a sneak preview of
Book #1:

TOO MANY BOYS!

Show it to your little sister, too!

"Have you ever been kissed?" I asked my twin sister, Allie, as I contemplated the open magazine in front of me.

She shot me a look of disgust from our closet where she was pawing through her wardrobe, flinging clothes out onto her bed. "No, Becky. I just beamed down from the planet Lovetron where we show affection by drooling on a guy. But only if he's a real babe."

"I wasn't actually *asking* you," I explained. "I was giving you a quiz from *Teen Life* magazine. It's called "Are You Ready for a Serious Relationship?" I scanned the test questions. "Hmm, here's another good one. 'If you're going steady with a guy, do you find it hard to turn down dates with others?'"

"I'm fourteen years old," Allie said, flinging a red miniskirt onto her bed. "I don't want to go steady." She turned to look at me. "You, on the other hand, are practically married, which is totally disgusting." She turned back to the closet. "Do you realize we have nothing to wear to this thing? I'm going to go ask Dad if we can have the credit card to go shopping."

The "thing" she was referring to was our first day as counselors-in-training at the new day camp at the Sunset Island Country Club. There were eight of us who'd been picked to be junior C.I.T.s and all of us were going into the ninth grade in the fall. There were also six senior C.I.T.s, all going into tenth grade, and ten counselors who would all be juniors and seniors in high school. The campers would be between the ages of five and twelve.

It wasn't really our idea to become C.I.T.s, to tell you the truth. I mean, every summer we come to our house on Sunset Island—this resort island off the coast of Maine—to have fun, *not* to have responsibility! But Sam—that's short for Samantha

Bridges—our au pair, saw this sign up at the club and told our father what a great idea she thought it would be for me and Allie.

You may be wondering what an au pair is. Well, it's kind of like a glorified babysitter. Personally, I could just die. I mean, Allie and I are *fourteen*!! But Dad is under the impression that Sam's a good influence on us because we don't have a mother. Which is why at the ancient age of fourteen we have a live-in babysitter.

Please don't tell anyone. It's completely mortifying.

I should explain to you about the not-having-a-mother thing. We *do* have a mother. Somewhere. We just don't know where she is. She left our family when we were just kids. I think maybe she ran off with this younger guy, but Dad won't talk about it so I don't know for sure. Anyway, she left.

Okay, I admit it. I feel funny about that. And about the fact that she never calls. Or writes. Sometimes I wonder if I did something to make her mad. But then I remember that I was just a little kid, so what could I have done that was really so awful? Usually I try to tell myself it's my mother's loss, not knowing me and Allie, but sometimes it's hard, you know?

About me and Allie: Sometimes we're the best of friends and sometimes I hate her guts. Of course, if anyone else ever said anything bad about her, I would kill them first and ask questions later. We look exactly alike—on the short side of average height, nice brown hair (Allie's is a little shorter), decent figures, decent faces, I guess.

It's weird, though. Some days I look in the mirror and I think I am really cute. And other days I look in the mirror and I am certain I should wear a paper bag over my head because I am such a dog.

The only real way you can tell me and Allie apart is that I have a beauty mark over my lip, and Allie doesn't. Of course, we aren't exactly alike on the inside. Allie is always changing things about herself— like one day she wants to be a nun (and we're Jewish, so that is kind of bizarre), and another day she wants to be a modern dancer. One day she dresses really outrageously and wears lots of makeup, the next day she wears baggies and scrubs her face clean. Who knows why? She also loves to read, and I hate to read. Two of the things we do agree about are Sam and Dad.

About Dad. He's okay. I don't think it's so easy, being a single father. And sometimes he really messes up. Like he'll be really permissive one minute, and really overprotective the next. That kind of thing drives me crazy. But basically we know he really loves us, and we love him right back.

About Sam. I know how I said she's our babysitter and how excruciating that is, but the truth of the matter is, I really like her. She really is cool. She's nineteen years old, she's tall and thin, and she has this incredibly great wild red hair. She's been a professional dancer and model. And she's the funniest person I've ever met. She also has the hottest boyfriend—next to mine—on the face of the earth. His name is Pres, and he's the bass player for a band called Flirting With Danger. I suppose what I really wish is that instead of being my babysitter, Sam was my big sister. Not that I would ever tell *her* that. I figure it would look like a total suck-up.

I have to admit, I'm not always so nice to Sam. It's just that sometimes I feel so angry, like she's only paying attention to me and Allie because my father is *paying* her. I figure if it wasn't for the money, she'd be saying, "Becky and Allie *who*?"

And then she'd walk right out on us, just like my mother did.

Anyway, more about this C.I.T. thing. Sam told Dad what a good idea it would be for us, and he agreed right away. At first we were totally against it. But then we got to thinking: Wouldn't it be great for a change to be the ones telling kids what to do, instead of being the ones who got *told* what to do? Also, Allie and I like little kids. Allie likes all that nature-girl stuff, too, like camping and fishing. Yuck.

Dad decided that being junior C.I.T.s would build our character, teach us responsibility, and all that. So he made us an offer we couldn't refuse: If we got the jobs, kept the jobs, and did them well, he would number one: let us give an end-of-the-summer blow-out party of a lifetime, and number two: take us on a trip to Disney World.

Who could turn that down?

I watched absently as Allie buttoned up a cropped denim shirt and wriggled into a pair of cut-off jeans with lace patches on them. "Hey, do I look fat in these, Becks?"

Pulled from my daydream, I checked out her outfit. "It looks okay to me."

"It looks awful," Allie decided, pulling off

the jeans. "I mean, that look is so five minutes ago!"

"Gimme a break, Allie, it's camp, not a fashion show," I reminded her, closing the magazine and putting it on the nightstand.

"So?" Allie asked. "I want to make a good first impression." She sat down on her bed and stared at me. "Do you think the other kids will like us?"

I shrugged. "Maybe we won't like them."

"Maybe," she said, scuffing her stocking-feet into the rug. "I can't figure out what's right to wear."

"Shorts and a T-shirt?" I suggested.

"Yeah, but what kind?" Allie asked. "Baggie shorts? Tight shorts? Short shorts? And what kind of T-shirt? Plain? With a logo? Tight? Loose?"

"Well, we shouldn't look like we're trying too hard," I mused, which is what I figured Sam would say.

"Okay," Allie agreed. "We have to try really hard to make it look like we're not trying hard, which means we definitely need something new to wear tomorrow. Which means we definitely need the credit card. Hey, Dad!" she called, and hurried out of the room.

I threw myself down on my stomach, kicked my legs into the air, and stared dreamily out the window. Hopefully, this C.I.T. thing would be fun. The only bad thing about it was that my boyfriend, Ian Templeton, wasn't going to be a C.I.T. with me. I tried to talk him into it, but he wasn't interested.

Actually, he said he would rather eat nails, have toothpicks shoved under his fingernails, and then have his body covered in honey while red ants crawled over him in a feeding frenzy. I took that to mean that the answer was no.

Ian has much more important things on his mind than being a C.I.T. He may only be thirteen, but he is the head of an incredible cutting edge rock band called Lord Whitehead and the Zit People. Allie and I sing backup for the Zits. Is that cool, or what?

Ian is very, very serious about his music. That is kind of why I fell for him in the first place. I mean, I had always liked older, beefcake-type guys, and for a long time I ignored the fact that Ian had a crush on me. And although Ian is short, wiry, and bites his nails, he is an awesome musician and he's very mature.

Oh, and another thing—believe it or not, Ian is the son of rock superstar Graham Perry. Graham is so famous that he and

Billy Joel played a concert *together* in San Francisco! Well, Ian is just as talented as his father. Maybe even more talented. It may take a while for the world to understand his music, but it'll happen.

And then we will ride off together into the land of the rich and famous, and probably my mother will read about me in *People* magazine, and she'll be really, really sorry that she ever left us, and she'll call me on the phone and beg me to forgive her.

And then I'll say, "I'll think about it."

SUNSET ISLAND MAILBOX

Dear Readers,

I had a great time writing this book and introducing all of you to Erin Kane. The idea of having an overweight girl on the island who is cool, good-looking and confident came from a reader. So, as you can see, I really do use your ideas!

I'm very excited about the next Sunset book. It's called Sunset Magic and it will be in bookstores this July. In it, you'll find that major surprise that I've been talking about for a long time. I wish I could tell you what it is, but I really can't ruin the surprise. Let's just say that it's something completely new, something we can all be a part of, and that it's very much based on the letters I've received from all of you. After you get the Sunset Magic book, you've just got to write to me and let me know what you think!

I've also been having a blast writing the Club Sunset Island books. The first one will be in bookstores this month! This is another idea that came from readers. Do send me all of your ideas so I can write about the issues that really concern you.

I've gotten some great pictures from you guys lately—Lindsay Bostwick of Cincinnati, Ohio—you are a major cutie! Also Lori La Barge, Sherri Yost, Lauren Lyles, and Beth Glasgow. Hey Beth, thanks for sending me the theater review you wrote. Very impressive! I love getting photos from you guys, so keep it up!

Well, I'm feeling kind of philosophical for some reason, so I'll leave you with this deep thought. No matter how old you are, or where you are in your life, there are always problems and challenges. Some things you can change, and some you can't. But remember this: although you may not be able to control the hand you're dealt, you certainly can control how you play the game.

You are wonderful, special, and unique, and you deserve the best!

See you on the island!
Best-
Cherie Bennett

Dear Cherie,

I really love your Sunset Books. I've read them all! I really like the idea of one of the characters being pressured to do drugs, maybe one of the guys in the Flirts. I feel sometimes it's harder for a boy to say "no" in front of his friends than it is for a girl.

Yours truly,
Tiffany Lucas
Humble, Texas

Dear Tiffany,

I just heard a survey on TV which said that drug use is up among teens. For girls, one of the big problems with drugs—and I'm including alcohol in this—is that sometimes a girl uses them so she doesn't have to take responsibility for her actions (as in

"I was so wasted, I don't know what happened"). In my opinion, that is dumb and dangerous. It means giving away your own power—something you should never do. I'd love to have your input on this issue. When it comes to drugs, is there more peer pressure for guys or for girls?

Best,
Cherie

Dear Cherie,

I wanted to thank you so much for writing me back. I know in your books you always say that you'll write back, but I feel special that you wrote to me and that you seem so sincere. I can't tell you enough how much I love your books. I'm curious, what kind of books do you like to read?

Love,
Kimberly Ellis
Maynard, Arizona

Dear Kimberly,

Listen, I absolutely love getting letters from you and it's my pleasure to answer them. I read a lot of modern fiction. You mentioned that you love to read horror novels. I know they're very popular, but they just don't speak to me at all. The best two novels I've read in the last few years are Gone To Soldiers by Marge Piercy and She's Come Undone by Wally Lamb. So, write to me and tell me your favorite novels, besides Sunset Island books, of course. Happy reading!

Best,
Cherie

Dear Cherie,

I wrote to you and told you I want to be a writer, and you actually wrote me back! Well, so far, I've followed your advice all the way. This time I have a couple of questions for you. If you wake up in the morning and all you can think of is writing, are you a writer or is it just something you thought of first, like the weather? Also, do you write the story first or the title?

Sincerely,
Nina Juarez
Bay City, Texas

Dear Nina,

Congratulations! If you wake up in the morning thinking about writing, you have the spark! Now you just have to act on it! Many people talk about writing, but most people don't actually do it. You can be one of the doers! Don't let anyone or anything stop you. Don't let anyone say you can't succeed, because you can. Sit down and write every day. Make a commitment—the same way an athlete makes a commitment to her sport. Read all that you can. Keep your eyes open. Watch people. Write about what is in your heart. It doesn't matter if you think up your title first, last, or in the middle of your writing. Follow your dreams, and reach for the stars!

Best,
Cherie